# FLiRT

# VIPs

## By Nicole Clarke

GROSSET & DUNLAP
Published by the Penguin Group
Penguin Group (USA) Inc., 375 Hudson Street,
New York, New York 10014, U.S.A.
Penguin Group (Canada), 90 Eglinton Avenue East, Suite
700, Toronto, Ontario, Canada M4P 2Y3
(a division of Pearson Penguin Canada Inc.)
Penguin Books Ltd, 80 Strand, London WC2R 0RL, England
Penguin Ireland, 25 St Stephen's Green, Dublin 2, Ireland
(a division of Penguin Books Ltd)
Penguin Group (Australia), 250 Camberwell Road,
Camberwell, Victoria 3124, Australia
(a division of Pearson Australia Group Pty Ltd)
Penguin Books India Pvt Ltd, 11 Community Centre,
Panchsheel Park, New Delhi - 110 017, India
Penguin Group (NZ), Cnr Airborne and Rosedale Roads,
Albany, Auckland 1310, New Zealand
(a division of Pearson New Zealand Ltd)
Penguin Books (South Africa) (Pty) Ltd, 24 Sturdee
Avenue, Rosebank, Johannesburg 2196, South Africa

Penguin Books Ltd, Registered Offices:
80 Strand, London WC2R 0RL, England

Clarke, Nicole.
 VIPs / by Nicole Clarke.
  p. cm. — (Flirt ; 6)
 Summary: As *Flirt* magazine gears up for Fashion Week and its own celebrity-filled fashion show, the four interns face greater demands on their time and talents at the same time they are adjusting to their new high schools.
 ISBN 0-448-44395-3 (pbk)
 [1. Models (Persons)—Fiction. 2. Fashion shows—Fiction.
 3.Internship programs—Fiction. 4. Fashion–Fiction. 5. High schools—Fiction.
 6. Schools—Fiction. 7. New York (N.Y.)—Fiction.]
 I. Title.
 PZ7.C55433Vip 2006
 [Fic]–dc22

10 9 8 7 6 5 4 3 2 1

# VIPs

## By Nicole Clarke

Grosset & Dunlap

## chapter one

**From:** alexa_v@flirt.com
**To:** manuelaferguson@sola.net
**Subject:** update

*Querida* Mani,
*¡Ay!* Last week we all collapsed in a heap from doing the
impossible—finding new schools and putting *Flirt* on the
Net—and there's still more to do: FASHION WEEK is here!
Ms. Bishop is putting on a fashion show that everyone
wants to be in! They are pouring into *Flirt* to make nice
to her. This weekend I saw Keira, Clay, and Jake (not
together) in our offices! Of course, the Big Boss just told
us all of this at the last minute—and now it's up to *us* to
make it happen.

Until Fashion Week ends, there will be hundreds of
celebrities in NYC and I will have to find the time to snap
as many of them as I can. So maybe I will find El Torero
this time!

*Besos,*
Lexa

⟲    ⟲    ⟲    ⟲    ⟲

*Ay, que linda—how beautiful,* Alexa Veron thought as she balanced herself with one foot on top of the cream-colored stone wall lining the quad of St. Catherine's School for Girls. Her other foot was anchored—kind of—in the elaborate scrollwork of the wall itself. The metal bars set into the top of the wall prevented her from achieving a more secure position.

A photographer had to be flexible—in more ways than one.

She snapped another shot of America's Top Catholic Nun. *Paging Tyra Banks! Sister Pauline should be a fashion model.* The nun had creamy mocha skin; lush, full lips; and heavily lashed dark brown eyes with gold flecks in them—all of which Alexa could see larger than life through the viewfinder of her digital camera.

It was Alexa's first day of school at St. Catherine's, the strictest Catholic girls' school in the northern hemisphere—or at least in New York City. Within the walls of St. Catherine's, she was not Alexa Veron, hip *Flirt* intern, but Alexa Veron, high school junior.

When she had put on her ugly navy-blue-and-green-plaid uniform for her first day of school, she had

66 *Paging Tyra Banks! Sister Pauline should be a fashion model.* 99

felt a strange sense of déjà vu, as if she were back in Argentina—and on the verge of getting in trouble either for failing a class or pulling a prank of the truly *fabuloso* variety. Alexa was known throughout the parochial school system of Buenos Aires as the foremost expert on practical jokes. She had been strongly cautioned *not* to continue her career north of the border. One bad move and she was out of St. Catherine's—and onto a plane back home. Not that home was bad. It was just . . . not New York. Not *Flirt*.

And she was not making a bad move. She was working on an assignment for the double issue from Lynn: to capture unusual shots of attractive New Yorkers. Alexa had several pix on her memory card that Lynn had already told her she wanted to see, and Alexa knew Lynn would be thrilled by the Sister Pauline series as well.

Sister Pauline wore a white veil and a white nun's habit that reached the floor. All white meant that she was a novitiate in her order. That was to say, a nun who had not yet taken her final vows. She was essentially an intern, just like Alexa, except that Alexa was an intern at *Flirt*. *Flirt* was the Bible of the fashion world, which made its publisher, Ms. Josephine Bishop, rather like the Pope of same.

*Or is that blasphemy?* Alexa wondered, crossing herself hastily. *I'm sure Ms. Bishop would agree with the comparison. Well, pretty sure, anyway.*

Lining up the shot in the viewfinder of her digital camera, Alexa framed the good sister inside the Gothic arch that led to the library. Sister Pauline, the school librarian, was sitting on a wood bench reading a book. Probably a good book. Maybe even *the* Good Book.

Alexa chuckled at her own little joke. Then Sister Pauline shifted as if she might stand up. Before her movements ruined the shot, Alexa took the picture. The white habit against the cream-colored stone of the school's wall, her exquisite brown features—the composition was so wonderful that Alexa had the chills.

A voice boomed out with righteous indignation.

"Alexa Veron! What are you doing?"

*"Ay!"*

Startled, Alexa jerked hard; she lost her balance, grabbing at the air and tumbling backward into the grassy quad. She instinctively cradled her camera, but it flew from her hands as she landed hard on her back in wet grass and mud. The breath was knocked out of her and everything momentarily faded to a hazy reddish gray.

The next thing she knew, Sister Pauline was dashing around the fence, shouting, "Alexa, are you all right?"

Alexa raised her head. "My camera. Where's my camera?"

Sister Pauline dipped down and picked it up where it had fallen, about two feet away.

"I have it," Sister Pauline assured her, showing it to her.

"And I'll take it," said the owner of the booming voice that had startled Alexa in the first place.

It was St. Catherine's Top Nun, aka Mother Michael Joseph, the school principal. She was dressed in a severe black-and-white habit just like in *The Sound of Music*—or in Argentina, where many nuns still wore traditional habits. She reached out her hand for Alexa's camera. Sister Pauline made a moue of apology at Alexa and handed it over.

Mother Michael dangled Alexa's camera from the wrist strap as if she were holding a dead rat by the tail.

"Did you ask Sister Pauline's permission to take her picture?"

"No," Alexa said, "but I do have a model release form. I was going to ask her to sign it if we used any of the shots."

"*Used* them?" Mother Michael asked, with the same horror as if Alexa had just announced that she was converting to Buddhism.

"Um, *sí*? In the magazine?"

Mother Michael's lips parted, but no more words came out.

Sister Pauline steadied Alexa as she got to her feet.

"Is anything broken?" Mother Michael asked Alexa in a chilly tone.

"I don't know, Mother," Alexa replied, reaching out her hand for the camera. "Please give it to me and I'll check."

The Mother Superior clutched her camera between her hands. "I meant, is anything broken on *you*?"

## "'I'm fine,' Alexa said. 'I think.'"

"I'm fine," Alexa said. "I think." Except for the part of her that was freaking out. Clearly, Mother Michael was furious with her for *something*, but Alexa had no idea what it was. She had carefully read the school handbook and nothing she had done—so far, anyway—seemed to warrant the wrath of her school principal.

"We'll go to the nurse's office, just in case," Mother Michael said. "Sister Pauline, you may return to your duties."

"Yes, Mother," said the pretty young nun. She gave Alexa a look that Alexa could not decipher and headed back around the stone wall.

*Ay, don't leave,* Alexa pleaded silently, trailing the Mother Superior out of the quad and down an open-air corridor. She was sweating, both from the hot weather and from fear.

They came to an intersection. Two girls in St. Catherine's uniforms were heading toward them. Alexa recognized Mary Beth Garcia from her interview to get into St. Catherine's, and Mary Beth obviously remembered her. The girl with her was shorter, wearing her hair very cropped and gelled, which accentuated her big blue eyes.

The Mother Superior said, "Where are you two going? You should be in class."

Mary Beth pointed to her watch. "I have to take my antibiotics."

Mother Michael looked at the other girl.

"Headache," she murmured, looking down at the ground.

"Well, come along with us, then," Mother Michael ordered them.

The two fell into step with Alexa.

Mary Beth whispered, "Man, you're so busted. Sister Andrew called your name about fifty times."

"Sister Andrew?" Alexa asked, clueless.

"Our chemistry teacher," Mary Beth said. "You *do* know that class started ten minutes ago? Make that almost fifteen."

> **Man, you're so busted.**

"No way!" Alexa cried under her breath.

Mary Beth held out her wrist and showed Alexa her trendy beaded-bracelet watch. Alexa read the time off the face. *9:13? No es posible!* She had started taking pictures of Sister Pauline at eight fifteen!

The Mother Superior's heavy shoes clomped down

the stone hallway. Her black skirt blew around her ankles in a sudden gust of hot wind. Alexa's clothes flapped, too, and she realized the entire back of her skirt and white blouse were wet, and she smelled like mud. This was definitely not turning out to be a very good first day of school.

Mary Beth said, "This is Chrissie DeMarco." The girl bobbed her head at Alexa. "She hardly ever gets in trouble," Mary Beth added with a grin, "but I still like her."

"I hardly ever get in trouble because I'm that good," Chrissie shot back with a lift of one her heavily plucked blond brows. "You're interning at *Flirt*, right? It must be amazing to work there."

"It is," Alexa confided. "And it's *loco*-crazy right now. We're putting on a fashion show at the end of Fashion Week, and—"

"Alexa, let's tend to you first. You may wait here, girls," Mother Michael said over her shoulder as she reached a dark brown door labeled NURSE.

Mary Beth whispered to Alexa, "Good luck."

"Pray for me," Alexa quipped.

Mary Beth grinned at her, revealing two fine rows

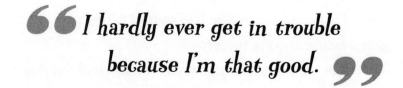

*I hardly ever get in trouble because I'm that good.*

of very straight teeth. She murmured, "No way. I'm an atheist."

Mother Michael opened the door to the nurse's office. The room smelled like rubbing alcohol. Another nun sat at a desk, typing away at an antiquated computer as big as a one-drawer file cabinet. She wore a white lab coat over her habit. She turned her head, saw Mother Michael and Alexa, stopped typing, and rose.

"Hello, Mother," she said. "What can I do for you?"

"Alexa fell off the wall," Mother Michael said. "I'm concerned about a concussion."

The other nun raised her brows. "Oh, my goodness! How on earth did you manage that? Well, come over here, dear." She gestured to a light brown examining table with a paper cover running down the center. "Just sit on the edge. I'm Sister Francis, the school nurse."

"I'm Alexa Veron," Alexa said, walking to the table.

The paper cover crinkled as Alexa climbed up the single step and perched on the edge. Her black flats dangled in midair.

"You're the girl from Argentina," Sister Francis said as she stood in front of Alexa.

"Yes, that one," Mother Michael replied.

Sister Francis cocked her head as she gently pressed her fingertips over Alexa's skull, moving around to various parts of her head as if she were searching for swelling.

"Any pain?"

Alexa shook her head. The sister reached into her lab-coat pocket and pulled out a pencil-shaped penlight.

"Now, stare straight ahead. I'm going to look in your eyes with my light. Try not to blink."

Alexa complied as the bright white beam came at her like a laser. "I feel fine. I feel ready to go to class right now."

"Class," Mother Michael intoned, "is nearly over."

*No. Maybe a third over, at most. There's a big difference when you're trying very hard not to get expelled.*

"I'm sorry," Alexa managed, shifting her weight. She felt squishy in her muddy clothes. "I lost track of time."

"Don't move your head, dear," Sister Francis said.

Mother Michael didn't respond to Alexa's apology.

That was not a good sign.

⊙      ⊙      ⊙      ⊙

Alexa passed the physical exam—no concussion, contusions, sprains, broken bones, or fractures. At Sister Francis's invitation, she slid off the examining table to

> **_She slid off the examining table to discover that she had left a huge, muddy butt print on the paper._**

discover that she had left a huge, muddy butt print on the paper.

Mother Michael looked first at it, then at her. Then she said, "Follow me, please."

*"Muchas gracias,"* Alexa said to Sister Francis, lapsing into Spanish because she was so nervous. *Please pray for me,* she added silently, figuring there was a good chance that the nun was not an atheist.

They swept into the principal's office—a place she knew from her interview—and Alexa stood diffidently while Mother Michael stopped in front of another door to the left of her large, dark wood desk. She glowered at Alexa, holding the precious camera in both her hands.

She said, "First, you skipped class."

Alexa held out her hands. "I didn't—"

"Second, you violated Sister Pauline's privacy. We are not cloistered—we mix with the secular world, obviously—but we do set ourselves apart. How many pictures of Sister Pauline did you take without her consent?"

Alexa had no idea. She hadn't even realized that

she'd been taking pictures of her for an hour. Time had flown. So had her shooting finger.

"I can tell you," she said. "I'll need to check the memory card—"

Mother Michael silenced her with another frozen stare. Then she reached into the pocket of her habit and extracted a brass ring of keys. Moving her fingers as if she were telling her rosary beads, she selected a key that looked to Alexa like all the others. She turned and jammed it into the lock of the door behind her.

She twisted the knob, the lock clicked, and she pulled the door open. A light flicked on and Alexa peered around the nun.

*¡Hijo!* It was a sizable walk-in closet with shelves from floor to ceiling. The shelves contained plastic bins, which were labeled with blank white strips.

Alexa had a very bad feeling.

Mother Michael picked a bin near the door at shoulder height and placed Alexa's camera in it. Then she grabbed a pen from a black cup on her desk with *St. Catherine's School for Girl*s embossed on it. She wrote on the label of the bin. Alexa couldn't make out the letters from where she stood, but she knew a confiscated camera when she saw one.

"When . . . when will I get it back?" she asked, crossing her fingers that it would be the end of school today. She had stuff on there that Lynn had told her to e-mail by six P.M. tonight.

"June," Mother Michael informed her.

ⓖ　　ⓖ　　ⓖ　　ⓖ

*From the Journal of Melanie Henderson*
*Monday, September 11*

*I'm writing this on a free period at my new school. I can't believe this is a public school! I'm loving it. Besides algebra II—trig, American history, P.E., and chemistry, I have poetry, intro to journalism, and a creative writing workshop. We're on the block system, which means that each class lasts an hour and forty-five minutes, and we have them on alternating days, except for Fridays, which is too complicated to explain (or rather, I'm too rushed right now!). I had poetry and journalism today, but I won't have my first actual creative writing workshop until tomorrow.*

*Today after school, I'm going to apply for a waitressing job where Liv used to work since the park job fell through (they don't have the funds right now). I really hope I get it. I need it. I need money, but I also need time. I'm already feeling jammed. We just read a poem about choosing your direction in life. I feel like I'm supposed to focus on ten different things at once. Like Fashion Week,*

*and the <u>Flirt</u> show, and our double issue, and—*
*There's the bell. Gotta go!*

       ☾    ☾    ☾    ☾

**FROM THE BLOG THAT ATE JAPAN!**
**OF KIYoKO!! GRRL WONDER!**

*saving flirt magazine one day at a time!!*
Written on: September 11 (first day of
school!)

1.  Jo Bishop is insane. We are
    now working on:
    • The double holiday issue
    • Fashion Week (eek!)
    • The *Flirt* Show—the big
    cockamamie fashion show for
    Fashion Week that she
    dreamed up over six months
    ago and *hello*? Could she have
    bothered to tell us about it
    when she begged us to stay for
    the school year?
2.  Not to worry! We are on the
    job! Go, Team Interns!
3.  My school. It's just as crazy
    as the rest of my life. All these

languages going all at once.
It's the Tower of Babel!
I brazenly thank whatever
superior being lurks above for
my iPod!
**Mood:** surly, moving toward
optimistic
**Music:** "Back to Bedlam," James Blunt
P.S.!!! THIS JUST IN! MY BIG SISTER MIKO
& HER SUPERMEGAFAMOUS GALPAL LILY
ARE COMING TO NYC TO BE IN **OUR**
FASHION SHOW!

☾     ☾     ☾     ☾

*The food is great,* Melanie Henderson thought, looking for that silver lining as she left Moe's. Her arms were filled with bags of takeout for the loft, and she was seriously anxious that she would drip the sauce that accompanied the Tofu Casserole Supreme all over her beaded top and embroidered flared jeans. The outfit was a wonderful back-to-school donation from *Flirt*'s famed Closet, courtesy of Jonah Jones.

*And I can walk to work*—which would be easier without the takeout, although she'd probably still have to bring her backpack. She could pack her cross-trainers and change into them for work. She certainly couldn't wear the strappy sandals she'd chosen for her first day of school.

*And it will be interesting to work at the same restaurant where Liv did her waitressing stint.* Liv had told her a few stories about some of the regular customers. Now she would get to see them up close and personal. Lots of NYU students ate there. And she was thinking about going to NYU, maybe. So there were several reasons to be excited about her new job.

*But I'm not excited, I'm relieved,* Melanie thought honestly as she walked down Mercer and headed for home. Around her, the rush and swirl of New York City on a warm afternoon underscored the pressure she felt. *I wish I didn't have to get a job. My homework is unbelievable. And then there're all the things I'll have to do at* Flirt.

She walked past the little pocket park and a brick building with the purple NYU flag and reached her building, which was six stories tall. She was living in the funky SoHo loft owned by *Flirt* magazine megamogul, Josephine Bishop, with five of the six original summer interns.

The sixth, Olivia Bourne-Cecil, had moved into Ms. Bishop's townhouse, her parents' requirement in return for allowing her to stay on for the school year. The interns had done such an impressive job that Ms. Bishop had asked them to stay on past summer. Such a thing had never happened before in the history of the program—and four of the six, the out-of-towners, had had to scramble to find schools and, in Mel's case, a job.

Mel hadn't been certain if she should stay. She'd had her junior year back in Berkeley all planned out—her classes as well as her after-school activities—and she missed her friends and family terribly. Especially her mother. She and her mom were practically the Gilmore Girls, more like friends than mother and daughter. It actually physically hurt to be separated from her.

"Hi, Sammy," she called as she squeezed through the green metal door. The hottie doorman looked way too warm in his maroon uniform with gold piping. He had a little fan on top of his bank of video monitors; when things were slow, he watched *Lost* and *Veronica Mars* or read science fiction novels. Kiyoko was teaching him Japanese, which was interesting, because her first language was pretty much Portuguese. She had lived in Brazil for much of her early life.

"Whoa, you're overloaded," Sammy said, rising from command central. He crossed to her and reached for the bags of takeout.

"Thanks, but I've got it all organized, kind of," she said. The weight of the bags was counterbalancing the weight of her backpack. She felt like Quasimodo. She had a ton of textbooks in there.

He walked her to the distressed metal elevator door and pushed the UP button for her. "That could seriously hurt your back," he said, hefting her left backpack strap off her shoulder for a second. "Be careful, will ya?"

"I will," she promised. Sammy bobbed his head at her and returned to his post.

The elevator door shuffled open and Mel pushed the button for the loft. Then the door opened into the spacious main room of exposed brick, arched multipaned windows, and a glossy hardwood floor. The windows revealed a spectacular view of the city, which was a fairyland of twinkle lights in the dying afternoon sun.

Before Mel, in the sunken living room, Kiyoko was pacing in front of the couch where Alexa sat, clutching an Indian-print throw pillow in her lap. Kiyoko had on one of her many anime T-shirts, a miniskirt that appeared to be made out of cherry red plastic, and red Chinese slippers. Alexa, in maroon jammie bottoms and a gray fleece sweatshirt that said *Gaucho* in scrolled letters, was near tears.

"There must be something we can do!" Kiyoko exclaimed.

Alexa raised her head and said wanly, "*Hola*, Mel."

"What's going on?" Melanie asked. "What's wrong?"

"The big kahuna nicked her camera," Kiyoko said. "Heartless puffin."

"Penguins. We call them penguins," Alexa said into the pillow.

Mel raised her brows as she shifted the brown bags. "Translation?"

"I was taking some pictures of this beautiful nun, Sister Pauline," Alexa said, raising her head. "She's our librarian. And it turns out that that's forbidden, especially when you're doing it when you should be in chemistry class."

"Oh, Lex," Mel groaned. "Not good news."

"You're not helping, mate," Kiyoko remonstrated Mel. Then she stopped pacing and her dark brown eyes widened as she really looked at Mel. "And oh, my stars, is that takeout from your new place of employment?" Kiyoko had a friend who'd worked at Moe's—alas, no longer—which was how Olivia had gotten the job there in the first place.

Mel nodded. "I thought we should celebrate my new job."

"Oh, how brill!" Kiyoko cried. "Did you bring enough for four? Liv's popping round to tell us about her first day at the Ooh-la-la-chichi School for Sheltered Rich Girls."

"Excuse me, but I go there, too. And *five* people live here, making a total of *six* for dinner," said a voice from the metal twisty staircase that led to the bedrooms. It was Jo Bishop's gorgeous dark-eyed, dark-haired niece, Gen, followed closely behind by her Mini-Gen, the curvaceous Charlotte.

"*No hay problema* if you didn't get enough," Alexa moped. "They can have mine. I'm not hungry."

"I brought plenty," Mel assured everybody. Then she turned her attention back to Alexa. "Now, please start over. Did someone steal your camera?"

"Yes," Kiyoko said emphatically, at the exact same time that Alexa said, "No."

Kiyoko walked up to Mel with her arms open. Melanie handed her a sack brimming with fragrant Tofu Supreme and a tub of brown rice. Kiyoko carried it into the funky retro fifties kitchen area and set it on the Formica counter.

"Not exactly. Mother Michael put it in the closet of no return until June," Alexa told her. "And I have shots on that camera that Lynn wants *tonight*."

Mel said, "Well, if you just explain that you need it for work—"

"I tried. She couldn't have cared less," Alexa replied. "And no, I don't have backups of the pictures; and yes, Lynn knew which other shots she wanted off the card, so I can't replace the card without telling her."

Mel was aghast. "Doesn't Mother Michael believe in second chances?"

Alexa threw back her dark hair. "As far as she's concerned, allowing me into St. Catherine's *was* my second chance. Since I had messed up so badly back in B.A."

"That totally stinks, as we say in J-A-P-A-N," Kiyoko chimed in.

"On top of everything, it's possible that my camera was broken," Alexa continued, her face crumpling. "She wouldn't even let me check."

Mel said, "I think the first thing you should do is e-mail Lynn and tell her . . ." She hesitated. *Should* Alexa tell her the truth?

"Tell her that someone *else* stole your camera," Gen suggested. "Then it's not your fault."

"I should have uploaded the pictures last night, just like I planned to," Alexa told the pillow.

"Well, it seems to me that the obvious thing to do is bribe the janitor to open the closet and take out your memory card," Kiyoko said, standing at the entry into the kitchen with a serving spoon and an opened container of takeout.

"Hey, that's group food," Gen said as she and Charlotte came down the stairs.

"I'm taking one little taste. With an enormous spoon," Kiyoko assured her.

Then Mel's cell phone trilled. Moving fast, she slung her backpack onto the brick floor and unzipped the pocket where she kept her purse. She dug in and retrieved the phone, but by then her voicemail system had taken over. As soon as it beeped, she listened to the message.

"Melanie, Jo Bishop. I need you at *Flirt* by five. We have copy to go over."

Mel winced, in part because she had missed her boss's call. "I have to go to over to *Flirt*." She'd been hoping she could work from the loft.

"What is it? Fashion show or double issue?" Charlotte asked. "Trey is driving me crazy, too. We're trying to get podcasts with all these celebs who are here for Fashion Week."

Charlotte had recently gotten transferred from not-quite-as-cool-as-the-other-departments Health and Fitness, to the hottest internship there was in the brand-new electronic content division. Kiyoko's former mentor, Trey, was now Charlotte's boss, and Kiyoko worked for Belle Holder, the world-famous music journalist who had gotten hired on to head Entertainment. Kiyoko's internship was probably second-hottest. For Kiyoko, that was a problem on a footing with global warming.

"Yeah, we're in on that," Kiyoko said, sounding a little edgy. Mel knew Kiyoko practically broke out in hives if it looked like she might miss out on something cool. She waved her spoon, "Guess who we're having dinner with tomorrow night." She waited until she had everyone's attention. "Kanye West!"

"Omigod! Are we going, too?" Charlotte asked. "I love his stuff!"

"You'll have to talk to Belle about that," Kiyoko said, the edge sharpening.

Mel was bummed. She liked peace and harmony. She kept hoping that after three months of living together, everyone would have figured out by now how to get along. But the changes at *Flirt* had caused new ripples in the dynamics among the interns, and so far, they were not all so good.

"Is it just me," Mel said, "or does it seem like the minute we all decided to stay here, the pressure on us at the magazine went way up?"

"It's not just you," Kiyoko said. "Now, back to bribing the janitor."

"We don't have a janitor," Alexa said, despairing. "We have a cleaning service."

"I can work with that." Kiyoko took another spoonful of tofu.

"Double-dipping!" Gen cried, pointing a finger at her.

"*Shitsurei shimashita,*" Kiyoko said, bowing and chewing. "Mel's right. I'm under too much pressure."

Mel's cell phone went off again.

"I need my camera," Alexa wailed.

Then Charlotte's cell phone went off.

"Good grief," Gen said, rolling her big brown eyes. "This place is a madhouse."

**flyguyeli: Hey. U! How was school?**
**LondonCalling: Lovely. thank you.**
**flyguyeli: Homework 2nite?**
**LondonCalling: 1st. hello to girls.**
**flyguyeli: Me next?**
**LondonCalling: 6 pm in coffee place?**
**flyguyeli: I'll be there.**

Liv Bourne-Cecil was still dressed in her dark gray and hunter green school uniform when she arrived at the building she had once called home.

After a lurching ride through traffic, she was at her old building. She greeted Sammy and caught the lift; now, as the door opened into the loft proper, Gen Bishop cried out, "This place is a madhouse!"

*But it's home,* Liv thought wistfully.

"Hello, everyone," Liv said, feeling a weight float off her shoulders as she gazed at the faces of her friends. Since her parents had insisted she move in with Jo Bishop, she had missed the other girls dreadfully.

*"Hola,"* Alexa said from the couch. But she was not her usual bubbly chica-snappa self.

Mel was on the phone. She nodded at Liv as she said, "Yes, Mom, school was great. Tell everyone I love them."

Mel disconnected with a soft smile that suggested to Liv that the Cali girl was a little homesick. She said, "Liv, hi. How was school? There's supposed to be a car downstairs. Did you see it?"

"No," Liv replied. "School was fantastic," she said, aware that Gen was listening. "Yours?"

"I love it." Grinning broadly, Mel pushed her hair away from her forehead as she bent down to pick up her backpack. She carried it toward the twisting metal staircase. "I'm going to learn so much. I got the job at Moe's, too. I brought takeout to celebrate."

"Oh, brilliant!" Liv said, following Mel up the stairs and into the room Mel shared with Gen.

Of all the girls, Liv related to Melanie the best. Perhaps that was because Melanie was an intellectual, and she was a little less noisy and dramatic than Alexa and Kiyoko. Not that Liv disliked those qualities in her two friends. It was just that, as an introverted Brit, she found them a bit wearing at times. Or used to—now she missed the noise and chatter. It was very lonely at Jo Bishop's townhouse. Ms. Bishop was never home.

"Working in a restaurant will be better than the park," Liv counseled Mel, as Mel dumped her backpack by her desk, unzipped it, and retrieved her purse. "Tips, you know."

Mel soldiered up a smile, but Liv could see that Melanie was making the best of a difficult situation. Now that Liv's parents had reinstated her funding, she had trouble believing she herself had actually held down a waitressing job and interned at the same time. It was incredible that Melanie would be doing that *and* going to school as well.

"Tips will be good," Mel said. She stretched her arms over her head, then lowered her upper torso to the floor. Her honey blond hair hung down like a waterfall. "I'm so jammed. I need to meditate. Maybe I should find a yoga class."

Liv suppressed a chuckle—Mel was *such* the Northern California hippie chick.

"Perhaps I'll join you," Liv suggested.

"As if I had the time, or the money. Seriously, how was your school?" Mel asked again, knowing Liv's previous answer was for the benefit of Gen and Charlotte.

"Quite nice, actually," Liv replied.

As Mel straightened back up, Liv smiled at her friend, and they went back down the circular staircase to the main loft space. Charlotte was still talking on her cell phone.

Gen was seated in an overstuffed chair catty-corner to Alexa. She had a book propped on her knees and she was listening to her iPod. When she saw Liv, she pulled one earphone off and said, "Liv, Charlotte and I missed you in AP French today." Her hesitation bordered on theatrical as she added, "You *are* in AP, right?"

"Oh, French," Liv said. Her cheeks went pink. "Well, you see, I passed my O level back home in London, so I don't have to take it."

"That's European for she's blasted past you," Kiyoko explained, chewing thoughtfully as she leaned against the doorjamb with legs crossed at the ankle.

Gen turned a choking shade of purple. Liv almost felt sorry for her. Jo Bishop's niece was a classic poor little rich girl—a sort that Olivia was intimately acquainted with. Many of the girls she knew in London were the same.

At the beginning of the summer, Gen had thoroughly intimidated Mel and Alexa, along with her "best friend," Charlotte. However, over time, the girls had come to realize that there wasn't a whole lot of love between Gen and her aunt . . . and that Ms. Bishop regarded everything Gen told her with a healthy dose of skepticism. That significantly reduced her power to bully the others. Even Charlotte, her first lieutenant, was beginning to mutiny.

"This needs more *shoyu*. Soy sauce." Kiyoko went back into the kitchen.

Charlotte flipped her cell closed. "That was Trey," she said. "He's e-mailing me some podcast stuff to work on tonight." She grimaced. "And I *am* taking French, and I have a ton of irregular verbs to memorize."

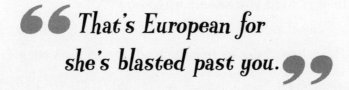

**66 *That's European for she's blasted past you.* 99**

**"What is it with all these people?"**

"He *does* know you're back in school, right?" Kiyoko called from the kitchen. "What is it with all these people?"

Liv said, "I'm looking forward to my studies. But I honestly don't know how we're expected to keep up with our schoolwork and do our internships properly."

"Well, Aunt Jo would tell you to prioritize," Gen said.

"We know about the prioritizing thing. We've worked for the old girl for three months," Kiyoko snarked, coming back out of the kitchen. She was carrying a liter bottle of Calpico, a Japanese beverage she couldn't seem to live without lately. They had it in London, where they called it Calpis. Taking a swig, Kiyoko gazed cross-eyed at Alexa. Then she lowered the bottle, smacking her lips.

"So, at midnight we break into your school dressed like ninjas and liberate your camera, yes?"

"And we get caught and I get sent back to Argentina?" Alexa said. "No."

"You need a Plan C," Mel said, "but you guys will have to figure it out without me."

"Plan C?" said a masculine voice from down the hall. "What are you vixens up to now?"

Liv watched Melanie's crimson flush work its way up from her chest to her neck to her face as Nick Lyric, son of their housemother, strode into the room. He had on a paint-splattered T-shirt and baggy painter's pants that drooped around his hips. He was handsome, Liv had to give him that. Mel fancied him, but she was also aware that he was on the rebound from his breakup with Anastasia, and therefore not in a prime position for a new relationship—despite his and Mel's lusty midnight kiss the week before.

*Good on Mel for recognizing that,* thought Liv.

A bit flustered, Mel said, "The Mother Superior at Alexa's school confiscated her camera until June, and she needs some shots she took. And I have to go."

"Take some takeout," Kiyoko said, thrusting a white cardboard container at her. "I haven't eaten out of that one."

"Thanks, Kiko," she said, taking the container. She pushed the button for the elevator and moved her neck in a slow circle.

"You look tired," Nick said, concerned. His voice was warm and his body language screamed *I think you're hot, Melanie Henderson.* Perhaps unaware of how obvious his lust for her was, he added innocently, "Did you start your new job today?"

"I just filled out the paperwork today," Mel told him. And *her* body language screamed, *Come into the elevator with me so we can steam it up!*

"I start tomorrow," she continued, with just as much friendly diffidence.

"Busy lady," he said. *Want a foot rub? Want a massage? Want to take a nap with me?*

"Yeah." She sighed. *Rub my shoulders. Kiss the back of my neck. Kiss me all over.*

Then the lift arrived, the door opened, Mel said, "Bye"—*Now that I've seen you, I feel just like I drank a Red Bull!*—and left.

Liv hid her knowing grin as Nick turned to Alexa and said, "I have a camera you can borrow."

Alexa's smile was truly a heroic effort.

"*Gracias, compadre*, but I also need what's *in* the camera. Lynn wants to look at some of my shots. And they're on the memory card."

"Maybe if you explain to Lynn . . ." Nick said.

Alexa shook her head.

> ## " Alexa's smile was truly a heroic effort. "

Gen said, "The last thing she needs is anyone at *Flirt* knowing that she's already in trouble at school."

Charlotte gave her a look. "So it'll be our little secret, right?" she asked pointedly.

"Oh, of course," Gen said, smoothing her dark hair. She was very pretty. Unfortunately, she was also short, which made her dream of becoming a model rather impossible. On that account Liv felt for her, despite the fact that Gen was so difficult to get along with.

Then a spooky sort of tango trilled from the room that Kiyoko and Alexa shared, and Kiyoko said, *"Zut alors!* The leitmotif of the Codaceous one. Sixth time he's called in the last twenty-four hours." She grinned at them. "Give the lad an unlimited calling plan, and he's as chatty as a DJ. Especially if *I'm* on the other end."

ⓖ     ⓖ     ⓖ     ⓖ

"You have reached a number that has been disconnected or is no longer in service," Kiyoko said to Cody after she blasted into her room.

"You are not going to believe," Cody replied, "who's coming to New York with me."

Without giving her a chance to guess, he went on. "Matsumoto and Kanno. You are not going to believe *this,* either," he said excitedly. "We're providing the music for Yuko Sato's show in Fashion Week!"

Kiyoko did a happy dance. Shinichiro Matsumoto, a director-god in the world of anime, and Jiro Kanno, his composer, were Kiyoko's idols. And Yuko Sato was one of the most famous designers in all of Asia. Supplying the music for her show during Fashion Week was an

**"You have reached a number that has been disconnected or is no longer in service.""**

unbelievable coup.

"Cody, I can't believe it!"

"Neither can I!"

"We're geniuses! Manga psychedelic will conquer the known universe! We're going to be rock stars, my lad! Let's plan our outfits. Yoko Ono always wears a yellow jacket, have you noticed that?"

"Oh." Cody's voice dropped.

Kiyoko frowned. " 'Oh?' What's wrong? Don't you like yellow?"

"Ah."

Something was up. Something was wrong. Something was . . .

Then she knew.

"When you said 'we' are supplying music for Yuko Sato, that didn't mean me," she said slowly. "It wasn't the stuff we already came up with. You composed music for a client without me." She waited one agonizing second. When he didn't say anything, she closed her eyes and curled her lips back from her teeth like a rabid dog.

"Cody, that's *our* thing."

"Kiyoko, we already sold all our cues to Matsumoto and Kanno. We couldn't resell them."

"Unless they gave us permission. And what better

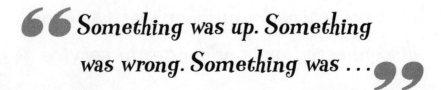

66 *Something was up. Something was wrong. Something was . . .* 99

way to drum up some financing for the project than to have the music playing during Fashion Week?" she said.

"It happened so fast," he said, almost as if he hadn't heard her. "Mariko—that's Yuko's daughter—came to the studio and said that they wanted some music. And Kanno and I just started jamming. We e-mailed it to Yuko and she loved it. And that's it. One pass, a few tweaks, and they bought it."

"But . . ." Kiyoko ran her hand through her hair as she fumbled for the correct words in English: *thief, hideous betrayer, pudding-headed lout. And how well does he know Yuko, anyway?*

"I thought you'd be here by now, Kiko." He paused. "You were supposed to fly back here so we could get started on the project. But . . . you decided to stay in New York so you could continue at *Flirt*."

"So you're punishing me?" she said. Her voice was rising. She and Cody had taken the bare bones of the street sound of manga psychedelic and made it their own. Together. They had taken it to her anime idols, Kanno and Matsumoto, also together.

"You should have called me immediately," she said. "E-mailed me, too. And let me participate."

Another pause. "Kiko, I—"

"Don't call me Kiko," she snapped at him.

He sighed. "We're coming in on Thursday. Yuko and Mariko will be at the W. I'm staying with Kanno and

Matsumoto at the studio. They can't wait to see you. They want to talk to you about *our* project."

She was a trifle mollified. But only a trifle. She said, "I have school, you know. And the W is passé."

"Ki . . . yoko, listen, please don't be so angry. You do so many amazing things." Cody's voice was low and quiet. "You've lived all over the world. I was a college student working for the summer as a disc jockey in a night club. What's happening, well, I never dreamed it would happen to me. I know I have you to thank for that."

"You were a disc jockey in a freeback club, which is even more pathetic," she teased him, softening a little. Belle Holder had forced Kiyoko to do an article on freeback, which Kiyoko had hated and considered even more passé than the W; it had turned into a podcast that *Rolling Stone* had been interested in. And her interview with Cody had turned into their collaboration, which had led to her second audition with Matsumoto and Kanno, after she had blown the first audition on her own.

*I hooked up with my idols because of Cody. I have to remember that. I have* him *to thank for that.*

"We have each other to thank," she said.

> ❝ **So, peace in our time?** ❞

"So, peace in our time?" he ventured. "I won't ever take another gig before checking with you first. I promise."

"Very well," she said

generously. "Peace in our time."

"I'll see you in three days."

"No doubt I'll talk to you in three hours. After I finish conjugating Portuguese verbs that end in *ir*. For God's sake, I *speak* Portuguese. This is such a waste of time."

"Maybe you can test out."

"Then I'd have to take something else. And I'd have to pay attention. Bishop has us hopping, lad."

Cody chuckled. "I've missed you, Kiyoko."

"Most people do, when they're not around me." She couldn't let herself say that she had missed him, too. Because that sounded too much like . . . what she had had with Matteo, the boy she had broken up with after she had met Cody.

*Just say it: My previous long-distance relationship.*

"Okay, well, I should go," Cody said. "You're probably juggling a million things."

"China plates, forks, and chain saws," she said.

"Your English never ceases to amaze me."

Kiyoko paused. "Peace in our time, Code Red, but I'm still a little . . . humph about the music."

"Okay. I get that."

"Kiyoko?" It was Olivia, who was standing in the doorway. "I need to go."

"Cody, I must sign off. Olivia needs me desperately."

"Got it. We'll talk again soon, *daijoubu*?" That was Japanese for "okay."

"*Daijoubu.*"

But as she disconnected and flung the phone on her bed, she realized that things really weren't very *daijoubu*.

"Listen to this. Tell me what you think," Kiyoko said. She told Olivia what Cody had done.

"Oh, Kiyoko, I completely understand why you're upset," Olivia said. "That was a musical style you developed together, and then he turned around and profited by it without you."

"It was loutish," Kiyoko confirmed. Her blood was warming again. "I'm not sure it's peace in our time. Maybe I should sue him." She flopped backward on the mattress and stared up at the ceiling. "Only I'm not old enough to sue him."

"Could you tell him you want some kind of credit?" Olivia suggested. " 'From a musical style developed by Kiyoko Katsuda and Cody Sammarkand?' "

Kiyoko sat up. "There's a thought."

Olivia smiled. "He'll make it right. He's a nice guy."

"One hopes," Kiyoko bit off.

They discussed their schools briefly. Kiyoko explained that the Manhattan International School was more of an "educational hotel," with floater students checking in and out all the time. There was a core group of the children of United Nations people, but Kiyoko suspected she had frightened them off somehow.

In turn, Liv told her that while she was a bit self-conscious about going to school with Gen and Charlotte, it was a nice school with an interesting study scheme.

"*Nice. Interesting.* Those are such Winnie-the-Pooh words," Kiyoko said. She meant that they were kind of nothing, but Olivia just looked at her as if she had lost her mind. That was how it usually went down between them.

"I mean, I'm glad you like your school," Kiyoko said, imagining Monets on the walls and a string quartet playing at lunch.

"Thank you. I hope yours turns out to be wonderful. Unless that's also a Winnie-the-Pooh word."

"Close," Kiyoko informed her.

"I see," Olivia said, but it was obvious that she didn't. Then she added, "I'm going to meet Eli now." The corners of her mouth shifted into boyfriend-happy, and Kiyoko was envious. She had never had a boyfriend she could just pop downstairs to see.

*Why is that, Kiyoko?* she asked herself. Guys were always flirting with her. She could have her pick of the litter.

*It's just bad timing,* she told herself.

ⓖ    ⓖ    ⓖ    ⓖ

"It's all in the timing," Belle said about two hours later, as Kiyoko followed her down a hall in the Hudson-Bennett building—past the glass cubicles and toward the more officelike offices of people like Hilda, Belle's assistant, which eventually led to the inner sanctum of Belle herself. It was hard to believe that Belle's office had been Trey's office not so long ago, and that *Flirt* had given her a generous redecorating budget that she had completely maxed out in two days.

"Timing. Check," Kiyoko said.

Belle nodded and kept walking, but Kiyoko wasn't sure her mentor was actually listening to her. While Kiyoko had been at school, Belle had punched her turbocharger into Warp Factor Five. She was moving so fast that even Kiyoko was having trouble parsing what she was saying and doing, and that was saying something. Trouble was, Kiyoko's attempts to either catch up with her or get her to slow down had been completely and totally ignored.

"We have more VIPs around here than they have at the Grammys, and that is just a slight exaggeration," Belle continued as they scooted past several assistants carrying mounds of clothes. Lynn Stein, Alexa's boss, was charging toward them from the other direction with two men in Savile Row–level dark gray suits and wraparound sunglasses, like Secret Service agents. They smelled like lemons.

"Gents, hi," Belle said, as they passed.

"Belle! We're lunching," said the guy on the left. He kissed her on the lips.

"Tomorrow at two," Belle confirmed, kissing him back, then turning to his clone and kissing him as well. Kiyoko watched in fascination, half-expecting Belle to kiss Lynn, too.

Or at least, to introduce them to her intern . . .

But such was not to be. Lynn and the blokes walked on, and Belle turned back to Kiyoko.

"An abundance of VIPs is extremely good. But we'll have to finesse all situations. Egos will be flying. You savvy?" Belle asked her.

"A little," Kiyoko said. She smiled sweetly. "English, you know, is not my native tongue."

"You're so full of crap sometimes," Belle said with a grin that took the sting out of her words. "What I'm saying is that we have to

**❝Egos will be flying.❞**

schedule these guys so each of them feels like they're the most important guy we have. They're all frickin' divas, but they're *our* divas, and that's a good thing. *Rolling Stone* is crazed that we're getting exclusives and they aren't."

Kiyoko was impressed. A month ago, Belle was writing the cover articles for *Rolling Stone.* Now she was their competition.

Kiyoko also had to hand it to Top Diva, speaking of divas. Bishop had managed to make an invitation to participate in the *Flirt* fashion show *the* hot ticket item for Fashion Week. Rock stars, movie stars, soccer stars . . . everyone who was anyone was scrambling to snag a walk down the runway, to present a fashion, to sing—anything. It was the ultimate "I'm cool" card. Realizing this as well, Bishop still had about half of the slots in the show open—so that the ego-driven celebs could lobby to get in. Top Diva was Top Dog, that was for sure.

Even cooler—to Kiyoko's globalized way of thinking—Bishop was showcasing designers, models, and makeup people from all over the world. A model from Rwanda, a Norwegian makeup artist, a designer from some Middle-Earth town in Wales—it was a mixture of the talented yet obscure and the mega-famous.

And Kiyoko's big sister, Miko, would be in their show, too. Brill!

"Kiyoko?" Belle said.

"Egos," Kiyoko said, pulling herself back to the moment. "Self-importance. Check."

"It's hard to get as far as these people do without a hell of a lot of drive," Belle went on. Kiyoko figured she could be talking about herself. Belle was a very ambitious woman. So was Kiyoko Katsuda.

"Drive. Check," Kiyoko said.

"So what we're going to do right now is go over our dossier on Kanye, nail down the basic facts of his life—feuds, ex-lovers, hits—and then we'll meet him at Nobu in . . . ninety," Belle said, glancing at a clock on the wall.

"Love Nobu. Love the caterpillar roll," Kiyoko said.

"Ah, but what does Kanye love?" Belle asked.

"I shall soon find out," Kiyoko declared.

"That's my girl." She looked Kiyoko up and down. Kiyoko had worn green silk walking shorts, yellow pointed flats, and a white silk-screened T-shirt of the Tokyo subway system. She was also wearing red enameled stop-sign earrings.

"Okay, you're good to go," Belle announced, giving her right stop sign earring a playful tap. "You get these in Italy?"

"How'd you know?" Kiyoko asked, lips parting, because of course she had.

"Pfft." Belle rolled her eyes.

*Oh, conversation is going well,* Kiyoko thought. *I should ask her about Cody. She knows all about him. She's the one who called Matsumoto and Kanno for us.*

"Listen, Belle," she began. "It's the funniest thing, but—"

"Hilda, sup?" Belle asked her assistant. She was seated in the anteroom to Belle's office with a headset on, and she looked kind of pooped.

Hilda said loudly into her headset, "I'm so sorry, *Ms. Carey*, can you hold one moment? I do apologize." She pressed a button.

"Mariah?" Belle queried.

"And there's someone in your office," Hilda said, as she nodded. "I thought it best to let him wait in there." She lowered her voice. "He thinks he's going out to dinner with you."

Belle blinked. "Okay." She turned to Kiyoko. "It starts. Watch a master."

"I am your admiring student, Yoda-*san*," Kiyoko assured her.

Belle picked up a sleek black portable phone from Hilda's desk.

"Mariah! Finally, we talk! You *are* coming tomorrow, right? I am so glad. Yes, it is a total drag that the Plaza closed. Oysters? Of course. We'll deliver some, and then I'll come help you eat them, good? Hilda knows where you're staying, right? You are the best!"

She handed the phone back to Hilda and said, "Make it so." Then to Kiyoko, "Okay. I'm putting on my game face."

Her expression didn't change, and Kiyoko cracked up.

Belle pushed open the door.

Kiyoko saw the tiniest little blip in Belle's composure. *Donato* was in her office. He of the bulgy biceps and twenty

> **He of the bulgy biceps and twenty or thirty kilos of tawny hair was the new god on the rock scene.**

or thirty kilos of tawny hair was the new god on the rock scene. He was rock history in the making. Kiyoko knew that every music editor of every magazine on earth would give years of their lives and/or pieces of their souls to be standing where she, Kiyoko Katsuda, was standing at this very moment.

Donato looked up from a copy of *Flirt* and smiled at Belle. He had a long, straight nose, no wrinkles anywhere, and there *had* to be some collagen in those lips. He was wearing black leather pants, a black T-shirt, and cowboy boots in this weather.

"Donato, this is so cool," Belle said calmly.

"*Bella* Belle," he said, putting down the magazine. He rose and threw open his arms. "I'm here!"

"You are the best," Belle said.

Just then, Hilda knocked on the open door and said, "Belle? So sorry, but someone from Maverick is on the line."

*Madonna's record company?* Kiyoko was about to swoon!

Donato gave Belle a funny little look, almost as if

he were daring her to take a call when he was standing right there. Kiyoko held her breath, wondering what on earth her boss would do. This was so wild!

⟳  ⟳  ⟳  ⟳

**From:** lynn_s@flirt.com
**To:** alexa_v@flirt.com
**Subject:** Photos

Alexa, I'm on a shoot. Charlanne Papel is coming in tomorrow c. 5:30 for her fitting. I want you there.

E me the photos off your card and I'll look at them from home tonight.

**From:** alexa_v@flirt.com
**To:** lynn_s@flirt.com
**Subject:** Re: Photos

Lynn, I am so sorry to tell you that my memory card is damaged and I cannot get the pix to send you tonight! I am very, very sorry!
Alexa

**From:** lynn_s@flirt.com
**To:** alexa_v@flirt.com
**Subject:** Re: Photos

Shoot wrapped c. eleven. Reading this from home, don't know if you're still up. Bring the card when you come in tomorrow & I'll see if I can get anything off it. I really want those pix!

Lynn

## chapter three

T*rite.*

*Timid.*

It was Tuesday morning, Mel was at school, and Ms. Bishop's withering couplet of adjectives was still ringing in Mel's ears. The scorn. The disappointment. Her boss had *hated* her first three drafts of the *Flirt* fashion show script.

Draft number one: "Where did my intern go?" Ms. Bishop had asked her, peering over the tops of her reading glasses as Mel stood before her desk like a condemned prisoner. "If you'd sent this in with your application, you would never have made it past the first round."

Draft number two: Bishop slashed at something with her blue pencil, gathered up all the pages, and thrust them at Mel.

"Try again."

Draft number three: "Just go home."

Mel had been so upset that she couldn't sleep.

"Okay, people, let's move into our groups." Ms. Kaneshige, the slender, dark-haired creative writing teacher in an ankle-length orange and red Gypsy skirt and putty-colored Birkenstocks, clapped her hands and started pointing to different sections of the classroom. The walls were painted a soft green and covered with posters of the movie versions of famous books: *The Lord of the Rings*, *Harry Potter*, and *The Chronicles of Narnia*.

At the beginning of class, the students had gone around the room, giving their names and the names of their favorite writers. Then they'd counted off into four groups and named their groups. Four groups of five or six meant there were about two dozen students in the entire class.

With the rest of her group, Mel grabbed up her backpack, her notebook, and her official blue editing pencil and schlepped everything over toward the dark green door. She figured the door was an auspicious sign— the door to her building was green, too—and smiled a little nervously at the rest of her workshop group. There were five of them—she was the sixth. The way she felt, there might as well have been five hundred.

One of the guys in her group caught her eye and smiled at her.

*Good morning, sunshine.*

His name was Jack. Charisma was pouring off him in waves. Some people were like that—there was

**"*That was the indefinable X factor Flirt was all about—that elusive quality of something … more.*"**

something about them that just caught and held you motionless, taking your breath away. That was the indefinable X factor *Flirt* was all about—that elusive quality of something . . . more.

This guy—Jack—had it. It started with his looks, which were a total combination of model-quality handsome with a fascinating edge: very curly dark brown hair streaked with gold, and eyes so blue they reminded her of the Pacific Ocean. The edge: a nose that was just a little long, brows that were much darker than his hair. He was tall and buffed out, and he had on long khaki board shorts and a white T-shirt with what appeared to be a line of Latin scrolled in black across his muscular chest.

But it went past his physical appearance. He had a golden, sexy warmth about him, as if he were keeping the best secret in the world, cuddled up against that great chest like a sweet little kitten. That secret was just purring with contentment, and Jack would be more than happy to share it with you, if you asked him. But you had to know you could ask.

And his welcoming grin—open, available—was telling Mel she could ask.

Mel's group claimed six newly vacated desks in their sector and began moving them into a circle. Still smiling, Jack sat across from her, slouching in the chair as he stretched out his long, tanned legs.

Mel's heartbeat picked up and her face tingled as

she pulled herself back into the classroom and got down to business. After they realized they all liked to write poetry, the group members dubbed themselves "the Poes." Ms. Kaneshige took that as her cue to deliver a lecture on Edgar Allan Poe's definition of a short story: a tale that produced "a single effect." They discussed what that meant for about twenty minutes. Then it was time to workshop. Everyone was supposed to bring a story to the first day of class for group discussion. After Mel's sleepless night processing Bishop's total hatred of her work, she wasn't much in the mood to get "discussed" again, but Ms. Kaneshige had picked her to go first in her group.

"All right, first readers," Ms. Kaneshige said. She glided over to the Poes and smiled down at Mel. "No need to be nervous. Workshop members, remember the rules we set up: Give specific, useful feedback. Be kind. Find something good to say. We're not interested in how *you* would have written the story. Help the author tell his or her story better. And readers: what else?"

"There's always room for improvement," Mel said along with the rest of the class.

"Right. Better doesn't mean it was bad to start with," the woman said. "It's good, better, even better."

*Unless you work for Bishop,* Mel thought.

"All right, please begin," Ms. Kaneshige said, drifting away.

"Okay, here goes," Mel said.

The other five shifted in their chairs and turned their attention to Mel.

Mel cleared her throat, and jumped off a cliff.

Then, just before she started to freefall, she glanced across at Jack.

He smiled straight at her, as if he knew just exactly how nervous she was.

*Yowza.*

    &#9685;    &#9685;    &#9685;    &#9685;

DJCody: So she did what????

Kiyoko_K: Belle told Donato she'd FINALLY managed to put him together w/ Kanye for that collaboration they were always talking about! Kanye was thrilled when Belle brought Donato to Nobu! They spent the whole dinner working on a song together. They got up and sang it and Nobu comped our dinner!

DJCody: Did BH plan it? Did she already know Donato was in her office?

Kiyoko_K: Unsure.

DJCody: Amazing!

Kiyoko_K: You cannot believe all the celebs pouring in. We came back to *Flirt* after dinner and I read off Belle's "While You Were Outs" from Hilda. Our *Flirt* show is hot, hot, hot!

DJCody: So are you, Kiyoko, :)

Kiyoko_K: Call me Kiko. Peace in our time. Since everyone has agreed to my credit!

DJCody: "From a musical style developed by Kiyoko Katsuda and Cody Sammarkand."

Kiyoko_K: Perfecta!

    ⓖ    ⓖ    ⓖ    ⓖ

Tuesday morning was hot and stuffy in the chemistry lab and *what* was Alexa going to do about her camera? She indulged in a brief fantasy starring her idol, El Torero, in which he swooped down from the wall she'd fallen off, elegantly burst into Mother Michael's office, and challenged her to a sword-fighting duel. He did not harm her, only sent her packing off to the Vatican. Then he sliced the lock right off the closet and graciously bestowed her camera upon his *enamorada, la hermosa Alexa* . . .

Sister Andrew whapped the periodic table with her long pointer.

*"Ay,"* Alexa cried softly, throwing back her shoulders and raising her chin, certain that she had been caught daydreaming. How could she be in trouble again already?

"That's absolutely correct, Mary Beth," Sister Andrew announced, her gaze lighting on the shaggy redhead, who was sitting directly behind Alexa. "A negative charge."

So Alexa was *not* in trouble, then. The nun had not been hitting the periodic table out of frustration with the fact that Alexa was beyond distracted. She was executing a victory *whap* for Mary Beth.

*What an unusual teaching style.*

Alexa tried to listen, but really, what good were protons and electrons on a day like today? She *had* to get her camera back before she went into *Flirt* that afternoon. Lynn was probably drumming her fingertips. Alexa could

**"What good were protons and electrons on a day like today?"**

pretend that she hadn't checked her e-mail last night *or* before going to school, but she was only forestalling the inevitable. Lynn knew that Alexa knew that she wanted those pix.

The only explanation she had come up with was that she had now *lost* the damaged memory card, and how lame did that make her sound?

Just then Mary Beth's foot tapped the rung of Alexa's desk and Mary Beth whispered, "Hydrochloric acid."

"Hydrochloric acid," Alexa said aloud, without missing a beat.

"Very good!" Sister Andrew beamed at her and whapped the periodic table again. Alexa jumped again.

Soon after that, the bell rang, signaling the end of chemistry. Alexa leaped to her feet, gathered her chemistry book and notebook in her arms, and crammed them into her backpack. Behind her, Mary Beth stretched and said sarcastically, "Well, that was relaxing. What is *wrong* with that woman, with all that hitting? She must have a lot of unexpressed hostility. Toward the no-dating-for-nuns rule or the heresies of Protestants or something."

"Thank you so much," Alexa breathed, looking at her. "You saved my life."

Mary Beth cocked her head, giving Alexa the once-over in return. "You're welcome. What is up with you? You're like a zombie that's had too much caffeine."

"I have a problem," Alexa said. As they walked with

the other girls toward the door, Alexa told Mary Beth what had happened yesterday, post-visit to the nurse.

"So your boss at *Flirt* wants your pictures and your pictures are on the memory card," Mary Beth concluded.

*"Sí."*

"And the memory card is in the camera, in the closet in Mother Michael's office."

*"Sí.* And it's locked."

Chrissie joined up with them. *"Hola,"* she said.

"Mother Mike took Alexa's camera. It's in the closet," Mary Beth told her. "She needs it for her work at *Flirt.*"

"If it's in the closet, she'll never give it back to you," Chrissie informed her. "Been there." She grinned, showing even white teeth. "Got it back."

"Oh?" Alexa took a breath filled with hope. "How?"

"Got the key," Chrissie replied, as if the answer were obvious. The three moved into the hallway and Alexa crowded in next to Chrissie.

"How did you do that?" Alexa asked. "The key is on a big ring. And the ring is in her pocket."

"Huh. It wasn't last semester," Chrissie ventured. "She kept it in this little pencil holder. I had this cool red scarf she took away from me. She said it violated our dress code." She scowled at the memory. Alexa saw then

# 66 Come on. You're an atheist.
## You don't believe in miracles. 99

that Chrissie had a temper on her. She was beginning to suspect that Chrissie was a fellow prankster.

"Pencil holder? Do you mean a little black thing?" Alexa asked, making a circle with her hands. "It says 'St. Catherine's School for Girls' on it?"

Chrissie nodded. "Yeah. She kept it on her desk. There was a piece of black yarn tied around the key and she just scooted the pencils out of the way and fished it out."

Alexa shrugged. "Well, she must have put it on her key ring this semester."

"Unless she has a duplicate," Mary Beth said. She smiled slyly at Alexa and Chrissie. "Maybe we should check that pencil holder."

"Maybe we should," Chrissie drawled, looking equally sly.

"It couldn't be that simple," Alexa managed, her chest tightening with hope.

"Why not?" Mary Beth challenged her.

"Come on. You're an atheist. You don't believe in miracles," Alexa said.

It was Mary Beth's turn to laugh. "I believe we make our own miracles."

"How could we do it?" she asked. If they were found

out, she would be suspended for sure. But if she could get that memory card . . .

"Oh, *please*," Mary Beth drawled. "Let's see. You need it by the end of school today."

"You could fall off the wall again," Chrissie suggested. Then she added, "Or I could get a headache."

"Good." Mary Beth narrowed her eyes and nodded at Chrissie. "A headache is good. Let's scheme, little *chiquitas*."

*Oh, my God! Are we the Three Amigas of Pranking?*
Alexa was thrilled!

ⓖ    ⓖ    ⓖ    ⓖ

" *. . . and it was like that old riddle about the lady and the tiger,*" Mel read. Her hands were trembling and she hadn't been able to catch her breath.

"*Except that no one knew what lay behind any of the doors, Anita least of all.*

"*She reached for the handle.*"

She stopped reading. No one moved. So she said shyly, "The end."

"Wow." Jack closed his eyes tightly as if absorbing her words into the very pores of his soul, then opened them again. "Yes." He smiled the Jack Smile.

Silently, Mel purred like that mystical kitten held closely against his chest. Starved for validation after

Bishop had ripped her to shreds, Jack's reaction was total catnip for her ego.

Another Poe—Matthew, freckled and sunburned—half-raised his hand. "I don't get it," he said. "So which door did she open?"

"I was kind of trying to leave that for the reader to decide," Mel replied with a sinking feeling. *I knew it. I knew it didn't make any sense. Jack's just being . . . sunshiny.*

"I think you should say that in the story," Matthew told her. "Otherwise, it's confusing. I didn't know it was over."

"That's the whole point," Jack said. He had a really thick accent that both intrigued her and cracked her up. He sounded like Tony Soprano. "It's *not* over." He smiled at Mel. "Yo, I wouldn't change a word."

A girl named LaToya said, "I felt like I was supposed to make up the ending, too."

"Art is *supposed* to demand participation," Jack insisted.

*He's calling my story art,* Mel thought, feeling yet more warm fuzzies.

Mel wished Jack were going to read next.

Across the circle, Jack gave his head a shake and mouthed, *Don't change a word.*

*I wish he were Ms. Bishop,* she thought.

*Wait. I totally do not wish that.*

## chapter four

Tuesday's lunch menu was spaghetti and meatballs, canned green beans, and applesauce. Back in Buenos Aires, Alexa would have had her pick of several entrees, and her school would never have served such terrible food. So maybe it wouldn't be too horrible to be sent home if their plan to get the key got them busted.

She, Mary Beth, and Chrissie had worked it out. During last period, Chrissie would get a bad headache and ask to go to the nurse. Mary Beth would get permission to escort her. When school ended for the day, Alexa would drop into the nurse's office to see how Chrissie was doing.

Chrissie's headache would be much worse, and Alexa would volunteer to ask Mother Michael to come check on her. Then either Alexa or Mary Beth would slip back out of the nurse's office while the other served as lookout, race into Mother Michael's office, and look for the key. What happened next depended on whether or not the duplicate was in the pencil holder . . . and on how long Chrissie could stall Mother Michael in the nurse's office.

It was risky, but it was the best they could do.

"You should eat something. Don't act all weird," Chrissie

urged Alexa as they sat beside each other in the dining room. It was in a lovely old stone building with arched stained glass windows depicting key events in the life of St. Catherine. "People will get suspicious."

"This *food* is weird," Mary Beth groused, seated across from Alexa. She twirled some spaghetti on her fork and watched it slide down the tines back onto her plate. "People will get suspicious if she *does* eat it."

After lunch came gym class. Yesterday they had gotten their PE uniforms. Today Alexa and the other girls changed into their regulation baggy navy blue shorts, white St. Catherine's T-shirts, blue socks, and athletic shoes.

Now they were being forced to play outside on "the court," a rectangle of blacktop softened by the heat. At either end, two orange baskets drooped like tired sunflowers. To separate them into teams, Alexa's side all wore blue plastic St. Catherine's wrist bands, which the school sold at fundraisers.

Sister Tobias, the coach, seemed to blow her coach's whistle whenever she felt like it, the way Sister Andrew slammed her pointer against the periodic table. Maybe Mary Beth was right: Nuns had to blow off a lot of steam.

> ❝ *Mary Beth was right: Nuns had to blow off a lot of steam.* ❞

The other side was winning, but no one on Alexa's team seemed to care one way or the other. Alexa certainly didn't. It was too hot, and lunch had been so awful, and—

"Fire down below!" Mary Beth shouted, as a bunch of girls screamed and scattered.

Chrissie was throwing up all over the place!

"Christine!" Sister Tobias shouted. She blew on her whistle as if that might stop Chrissie.

There was a pause in the action as Chrissie groaned. "Sorry, sorry," she rasped. "Sister, I am so . . . *bleah.*" She cupped her hand over her mouth.

Clearly vexed, Sister Tobias raised her whistle to her mouth, but didn't blow on it.

"Alexa and I will take her to Sister Andrew," Mary Beth offered, grimacing as she put an arm around Chrissie and started leading her away. She gave Alexa a hard look. "Come on, Alexa. Chrissie needs you."

*Oh my God,* Alexa thought. *We're doing it now. It's not going to be a headache. It's going to be vomiting.*

"Everyone leave the court," Sister Tobias ordered the class. "Class dismissed. Go to the showers." She gave her whistle another blast. "Alexa and Mary Beth, take Christine to Sister Andrew."

Alexa walked beside Chrissie, who was doubled over and moaning louder.

"Way to go," Mary Beth told Chrissie. "That was awesome."

"I'm really sick," Chrissie gasped.

"Well, your timing is perfect," Mary Beth congratulated her.

The three of them hustled down the corridor to the nurse's office. Alexa rapped hard, then pushed the door open and barreled through. Sister Andrew was at her desk, and Sister Pauline was standing beside the file cabinet with some magazines in her arms.

"Girls, what's wrong?" Sister Andrew asked.

"Chrissie's really sick," Alexa said. "You might need a bowl, Sister."

"It's gotta be food poisoning," Mary Beth said to Sister Andrew as the nun-nurse grabbed a silver kidney-shaped pan and handed it to Chrissie. "Maybe someone should get Mother Michael."

It was like a movie script. Or . . . a miracle.

Mary Beth looked at Alexa. Alexa looked at Mary Beth.

"I'll go," Mary Beth said.

And she was off.

Sister Pauline helped Chrissie lie down on a cot. Alexa got her a damp cloth for her forehead. Pale and wan, Chrissie flashed her a little wink and glanced down at her crossed fingers.

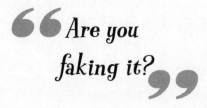
**Are you faking it?**

"Are you faking it?" Alexa whispered, as Sister Pauline went to get her a glass of water.

*"Please."* Chrissie shook her head. "But I *am* working it."

*For me,* Alexa thought, much moved.

Then Mother Michael rushed in.

Alone.

"Christine," she said. "How are you feeling?"

Chrissie raised up her head. "Barfy, Mother." Resting on one elbow, she sipped her water. "Maybe it was the spaghetti."

Mother Michael looked at Sister Andrew.

"It could be food poisoning," Sister Andrew said. "If more girls start feeling sick, we'll know."

Mother Michael sighed as only the principal of a private school that had poisoned the entire student body could sigh. Alexa did feel sorry for her, but she would have been even more sympathetic if she hadn't taken Alexa's camera.

"I'm going to call your parents, Christine," she said. Then, to Sister Andrew, "Please let me know how she's doing." She turned to go.

*Not yet! Mary Beth hasn't had enough time!*

"Oh," Alexa said, letting her knees buckle. "I'm not feeling so good, either." She draped herself into a plastic chair beside the cot and rested her chin on her chest.

"Do you need a pan?" Sister Andrew asked.

"*Sí, por favor*," Alexa murmured.

While Sister Andrew bustled, Mother Michael bent down, molding the back of her hand across Alexa's forehead, then cupping her cheek. Her skin was rough and dry. She needed some hand lotion.

"I don't think she has a fever," Mother Michael announced to Sister Andrew.

"May I also have a glass of water, please?" Alexa asked demurely.

"Of course. I'll get you one." Mother Michael straightened and swept over to a water cooler. She filled a paper cup and handed it to Alexa.

"Drink it slowly," Sister Andrew told her.

Just then, Mary Beth appeared in the open doorway. She scanned the room, saw Alexa, grinned, and gave her a thumbs-up. Then she disappeared.

*She got it!* Alexa wanted to scream, she was so relieved. She gulped the water down.

๏     ๏     ๏     ๏

Once she had decently "recuperated," Alexa left the nurse's office, showered, changed into her school uniform, and dashed to her English class. Mary Beth was there; she turned as soon as Alexa walked in. Her huge smile was a neon confirmation that all was well.

> **How incredible that a little thing smaller than two fingernails side by side could turn her world around.**

*Thank you, thank you, thank you,* Alexa beamed at her as she slipped into the empty desk beside her. Then she pulled out her English notebook and a pen, and tried to look attentive.

A few seconds later, Mary Beth discreetly laid the memory card on the lined page of notebook paper. All the tension and worry of the last twenty-four hours blew out of Alexa's lungs in one gigantic emotional purge. How incredible that a little thing smaller than two fingernails side by side could turn her world around.

*"Muchísimas gracias,"* she whispered, palming the card.

Mary Beth gave her a wave of her hand as if to say, *No big.* But it was a very big big.

*I am saved,* Alexa thought, delirious with joy.

ⓖ     ⓖ     ⓖ     ⓖ

The heat did not let up as the school day wore on. It wrung Mel out, and she was not looking forward to working a half-shift at the restaurant before tackling her fashion show script again. And her homework. At least she didn't have to go into the *Flirt* offices on top of it.

She stood at her locker, giving the script a read-through so she could think about it on the walk from school to Moe's. Ms. Bishop's blue checkmark next to *carrousel* rankled her. It was as if Ms. Bishop enjoyed finding things wrong with Mel's work.

Then she saw Jack, and she stuffed the script back into her backpack and slipped her arms through the straps.

"Yo, Mel, wait up," he said, catching up to her. "Walk with you?"

"Sure," she said, tingling from the back of her head to the base of her spine. He was *so* cute.

*Nick is cute, too,* she thought. And their kiss was also like a wonderful secret, catnip to her soul. She thought they might be starting to move to something new, now that he and his girlfriend had broken up and Mel was staying in New York. And they lived together. Not together together, but in the same place. That counted for something.

That counted for a lot. It also counted that he was Nick. Period.

"Carry anything for you?" Jack asked. *Your earthly worries? Your heart?*

"Got it, thanks," she replied in a not unfriendly way, and slammed the locker shut.

They joined the swirl of students headed for the exit. To Mel, who had always taken a bus to school, it seemed exotic to simply stroll out the front door and into the world.

"Another day done," Jack said.

"Actually, school is great so far," Mel said.

"I won't tell anyone you said that." Jack crossed his heart.

The crowd spilled onto the sidewalk. Cars whizzed past, kicking up layers of heat as if they were dust. She smelled the clean cotton of Jack's T-shirt mixed with a little bit of sweat.

"Listen, about your story. Those guys are wrong. It's perfect the way it is."

"There's always room for improvement," she intoned.

He vigorously shook his head. "Kaneshige is wrong, too. Stories are like bread dough. You mess with them too long, you kill the yeast. They won't rise and all that's left is a floppy pile of jack." He laughed. "Well, *that* came out wrong."

"No, it's nice. Thanks."

*And Bishop would totally disagree with you. She works it, finesses it, goes over and over it . . . and it comes out glazed, golden, and delicious.*

"You have talent," he said earnestly. "You can't go listening to everybody. You need to develop your own instincts." He gave her a lopsided grin. "And do I sound like a pompous jerk or what?"

"No," she said, and then she laughed and added, "Maybe just a little pompous. But not a jerk."

"I'm very opinionated," he conceded. "It's just . . . well, I've been in classes like this before. I've seen guys come in with something original and quirky, and then the workshopping begins, and everyone homogenizes it. Makes it sound like what they read in last week's workshop. Know what I mean?"

She shrugged, no mean feat with her backpack on. "I've never been in a workshop before," she admitted. Then she paused before going on.

She had given a lot of thought to whether she would tell the other kids in her new school about her internship. Part of her didn't want to be the object of close scrutiny. But the other part had watched Liv struggle with hiding the truth about herself from Eli—that she was practically English royalty—and she figured it was better to be honest from the get-go.

"But I am in New York on a writing internship," she said, feeling kind of cool as she said it. There was no denying that she wanted to impress him.

"No kidding," he said, stopping on the sidewalk. "Like, with a publishing house?"

"No. A magazine."

His mouth dropped open. She was loving this.

"Which one? I've submitted to a few. Never sold anything yet, but . . ."

*"Flirt,"* she said. "Do you know it?"

*"What?* Of course I do." He scratched his cheek. "I just . . . I don't picture you there," he said. "Um, no offense, but your story was very literary."

She got that. She had been just as dismissive when she had first come to New York. She had assumed she would learn what she could from "the fashion hacks" and apply it to her own serious, good stuff.

"It's really a great opportunity. I'm making connections and I'm working with the editor-in-chief herself. Josephine Bishop."

"I've seen her on the news a couple times," he said. "Seems kinda nasty."

Caught off guard—and realizing he was dead on— Mel laughed. "She's very demanding."

"Well, no offense, but demanding about what? Thirty lashes if you use 'persimmon' instead of 'orange'?"

"Or 'nectarine,' " she riposted. "Seriously, I thought that, too. But there's a whole art to putting the magazine

> ❝No offense, but demanding about what? Thirty lashes if you use 'persimmon' instead of 'orange'?❞

together. And we've got an amazing Web presence. We've got some great podcasts, and—"

"—and it's all to get women to buy clothes and makeup," he interrupted, looking intense. "That's the whole reason it exists." She saw him putting together his version of her life. "And you intern there, which means you work for free. Mel, you've got to be giving more than you're getting, working for them."

Mel was bummed down to her toes. He *was* a pompous jerk.

Bristling, she turned to go.

"Hold on. Something's sticking out of your backpack," he said. "It's caught in the zipper."

He gave the "something" a yank and showed it to her as she turned back around.

She recognized the third draft of her fashion show script. He skimmed the first page as he prepared to give it back to her.

". . . a sassy and chic filigree of a *sandal*?" he read.

"Yes. A sandal," she said, her cheeks heating. "Give that back, please. That's proprietary."

Grimacing, he thrust it at her as if it were on fire. "Oh, hey, I've pissed you off."

"Yeah, well," she managed. The light changed and she started across the street. She didn't know if Jack would follow. She didn't know if she wanted Jack to follow.

He called after her, "We'll continue this, all right?"

She moved her hand to signal that she'd heard. He didn't even realize how rude he'd been. All his earnestness on behalf of her talent felt patronizing now.

She walked on, thoughts of Jack and her story and her script tumbling around. Then she realized she had shot way past Astor Place and had to double back.

She finally sorted herself out and half-ran, half-walked toward the faded and torn green and white awning of Moe's. She spared a glance at the chalkboard showing the list of specials. Then she dashed inside, with no time for her eyes to adjust to the dimly lit interior.

First she bashed into a chair. Then she collided with another waitress who was, thankfully, only carrying a bin of silverware. It went crashing to the ground and Melanie cried, "Oh, I'm so sorry!"

She dropped to her knees and the weight of her backpack pushed her forward onto her hands. The other girl said, "It's okay. I've got it."

Mel made out shadowy knives, forks, and spoons. She clutched two handfuls of them, realizing she shouldn't drop them into the bin with the clean ones. So

**"He didn't even realize how rude he'd been. All his earnestness on behalf of her talent felt patronizing now."**

she sat back on her heels holding them up like a surgeon in the operating room.

Coming up behind her, Miguel, who had hired her, said, "You're late."

"And clumsy," the other waitress muttered.

Melanie craned her neck to look up at her boss. She could see his expression. He was not smiling.

"I'm sorry. I got a little lost. It won't happen again."

"Right," he said. "It won't."

For one lurching second, she thought he was firing her. Then he walked away.

"You're only working for four hours, right?" the other waitress said.

## chapter five

I *f it wouldn't cause a scene, I would gladly throttle Gen Bishop here and now,* Liv thought as she, Charlotte, Gen, and a few of Gen's friends walked across the commons after their last class of the day.

Gen had been regaling her friends with "amusing" stories about their fellow interns—selecting the most humiliating things she could think of to divulge, from snide comments about Mel's first hangover to her interest in Nick to imitating Kiyoko's unusual accent—but *only* "because it is just so fascinating."

"It's like living in a college dorm," Gen concluded with an airy little wave. "Or so I assume." She smiled at her little clique of girlfriends. "Speaking of college, I just had my first appointment with my placement coach. I'll probably be going to Yale. It's where my family goes."

Like Liv, Gen knew that Jo Bishop had not gone to Yale. She'd worked her way up from humble beginnings as an assistant at a design house in France. And *worked* was one of the key words—nothing was ever handed to Jo Bishop; she had never had one of those convenient "lucky" breaks bestowed upon so many other wealthy, successful people. She'd put herself through university one class at a time. She had an indomitable spirit and incredible backbone—and Liv admired her deeply for that.

Her difficult road was one of the main reasons Ms. Bishop had initiated the internship program—to give girls a real opportunity to learn about running a top-level fashion magazine. To have some direct experience with working with the best in the field, and to have a chance to make connections that would serve them well later.

Jo Bishop had always selected the interns herself, and she had picked this summer's six because she had seen something in their applications—a spark of talent, a passion similar to her own—that she felt she could help develop. And then, she had seen something even more special in each of them, and asked them all to stay on.

*At least, that's true of Kiyoko, Alexa, Mel, and Charlotte,* Liv thought. *But my parents are friends with Ms. Bishop. And Gen is her niece. So I'm not so sure about us.*

*Perhaps Gen also feels insecure about her place in her aunt's life. She's used to having her to herself after the summer interns leave. So she's cutting them down to size. It's quite unkind of her . . . and a little sad, really.*

She realized she'd lost track of the conversation when she heard her own name cross Gen's lips.

*My turn,* she thought. *I wonder what she has to say about me. If she makes fun of Eli . . .*

"We need to go," Liv said.

"Right," Charlotte put in.

Gen looked frustrated, as if she had more work to do, but she smiled and tossed her head, saying, "Right! It's just crazy at *Flirt* right now!"

Saying good-bye to the other girls, Liv, Gen, and Charlotte cabbed it over to the Hudson-Bennett building, which housed the offices of *Flirt*.

Liv was quite excited about Fashion Week. Last night, Demetria had told her that the first two hours of this afternoon would be full of sorting and organizing the clothes, shoes, and accessories for the *Flirt* show. Liv couldn't wait to see what creations Ms. Bishop's eclectic group of designers had come up with.

"Then Charlanne Papel is coming in for a fitting," she told her. "Five thirty. It'll be an event."

> **It'll be an event.**

No doubt. Charlanne Papel was a pop star on the order of Madonna or Donato. She was going to wear an evening gown designed by Gianna Russo, who was hot-hot-hot out of Milan. The dress had arrived by courier this morning, while Liv and the other girls had been at school. Liv couldn't wait to see it. Sketches had been faxed and JPEGed back and forth for weeks, and Liv was eager to see how the two-dimensional renditions had been transformed into a real garment.

*I'm so lucky to see this all firsthand,* she thought. *I'm soaking all this up as best I can.*

The three of them took the lift, Gen speaking in her

last name "B-I-S" to code it to go. Gen said to Charlotte, "Too bad you couldn't go with Kiyoko and Belle to Nobu last night. I know you really wanted to."

"Oh, it's okay," Charlotte replied, as she dug through her purse. She pulled out a tube of lip gloss and smoothed it on. It was a good tint for her. She, too, was learning on the job. "Trey told me we're going to mega-schmooze this week."

"Aunt Jo is having a string of private parties at her town house," Gen said. "Of course I'll be going to those."

Liv wondered if Gen knew that Ms. Bishop was having just such a party tonight. It was a private sit-down dinner for Gwyneth Paltrow and some other celebs. Ms. Bishop had informed Liv that she was expected to be there, but she hadn't said anything about Gen.

After leaving the elevator, they entered the long corridor of glass-and-metal cubicles, Gen turning right toward the Beauty suite of offices, while Liv made a left, toward Fashion.

Demetria's new assistant, a compact man named Dwayne, wasn't behind his desk, and the door to Demetria's office was closed. Liv prepared to knock when Dwayne hurried up to Liv and wagged his buffed fingernail in her face.

"No-no," he said, like a mother admonishing a toddler. "Do not disturb."

Liv raised her brows. "What's going on?"

"Big brainstorming session," he said, with an air of mystery. "Ms. Bishop has decided that there's no theme to the show."

Liv looked at the closed door. "I thought the theme was that it was eclectic," she said. "Designers from all over the world."

"She says that's messy." He wrinkled his nose as if he were smelling something unpleasant. "Lacks cohesion."

"Oh." She glanced at the door again. It seemed a top-level discussion like that would be something an intern should see. "Are you sure I'm not supposed to go in?"

He wrinkled his nose again. "No disturbez-vous," he said. "But she did tell me what she wanted you to do."

*Sort and organize the fashions,* she thought with relish.

"File," he said, waving her over to her desk. It was brimming with folders.

*"File?"* she echoed, shocked. "But what about Fashion Week?"

He shrugged. "All the more reason for us to stay on top of the little things, eh?" He reached down and scooped up a two-foot-thick slab of folders and dumped them into her arms. He pointed down the hall where the file cabinets were located.

Dejected, Liv headed in that direction.

Laughter rumbled from behind Demetria's closed door.

⊙     ⊙     ⊙     ⊙

"Oh my God," Belle said under her breath. "Kiyoko, go tell Jonah what we are seeing. I'll get a call through to Demetria stat."

It was four o'clock, and Belle had just finished discussing Kiyoko's "Kiko-Do" list. They were cool errands, consisting of attending to the whims of their divas, and Kiyoko was zinging with excitement to be off. Her fave item was delivering some Italian nougat candy to the apartment Donato was renting on Central Park West.

Kiyoko started to turn her head to see what it was that they *were* seeing when Belle murmured, "Don't look. Just turn around and start to walk. You will immediately understand."

*"Daijoubu,"* Kiyoko replied, and did as her mentor ordered.

*Oh. My. Nondenominational. God.*

It was the super-ultra-diva Charlanne Papel herself, ninety minutes early. She was surrounded by four bodyguards and three babelicious women, two of the chicks in jeans and T-shirts. The third was wearing a mannish suit. As she was six foot two, Charlanne towered above them all. Her black-black-black hair coiled around her sharp features like an old-fashioned bathing cap, accentuating her signature pencil-thin eyebrows and deep red lips.

She was wearing a bra-top and a micro-mini and Kiyoko saw the source of Yoda's concern: Charlanne had gotten herself a full-body tattoo of her own image, as some kind of wild crimson demon-goddess thing. It started at the base of her neck and tumbled into her top, plummeted down her stomach and into her skirt, then down her legs.

It was bizarre in the extreme—no less so because Charlanne was a pop princess, not some thrash-metal punk rocker. Maybe she had on body makeup, or a temporary tattoo for a photo shoot or a joke. But if it was permanent, it would completely overshadow the super-ultra-brill designer gown Gianna Russo had sent over just this morning for her.

As Charlanne and her entourage approached, Kiyoko bowed her head and sailed past in silence. Like the other interns, she had been coached to speak only when spoken to by the bevies of celebrities pouring into

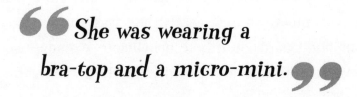

**She was wearing a bra-top and a micro-mini.**

the *Flirt* offices. Even eye contact was uncool. But it was very, very difficult not to stare.

As soon as Kiyoko was safely past, she picked up her pace to that of a charging rhino. She whipped around the corner and blasted down another hall en route to Jonah Jones, keeper of incoming fashions in his enormous suite of walk-in closets collectively known as The Closet.

She was running so fast she almost smacked into Liv, who was staggering beneath a leaning tower of folders. She put on the brakes and said, "Liv! Where's your leader?"

"She's in a meeting," Liv said, looking around the tall stack. "I'm not allowed in," she added, sounding piqued.

"My leader is calling her." Kiyoko put an invisible phone to her ear. "Red alert."

**66 My leader is calling her. 99**

"Oh? What's happened?" Liv asked.

"Come with me." Kiyoko grabbed Liv's folders, looked left and right, and dumped them into a mail cart, which was parked about three cubicles farther down the hall.

Then Kiyoko led the way to The Closet.

Seated on a tall stool, Jonah Jones, clad in ash gray silk trousers and an ivory polo shirt, was pressing a bottle of Perrier against his forehead. Busy assistants scurried around with piles of dresses, purses, and shoes. A second set of assistants carefully inserted beaded bolero jackets, black wool pants, and a scrumptious emerald green cape into cocoons of white muslin bags on hangers. White tags dangled from the necks of the hangers.

Liv said, "The sorting and organizing."

A dark-complexioned, harried-looking young woman was holding up a beaded evening gown as slinky as a snakeskin. It was Charlanne Papel's Gianna Russo original. Kiyoko had seen the sketches. The rose-colored beadwork was intricate, creating Impressionistic flowers that blossomed from sections of the dress, which was primarily made out of silver tissue. The bodice was nearly bare, just a strategically placed flower here and there. Charlanne's tattoo would look extraordinarily bizarre with it.

Jonah nodded approvingly and said, "Gianna Russo is a genius." To the woman, "Leave it out, sweetie. We're going to need it in a few."

"Or not," Kiyoko said.

"Girls," he said happily, as Kiyoko and Liv hovered in the doorway. "Isn't this the kick?"

"Houston, we might have a problem," Kiyoko announced. "A very interesting problem," she added.

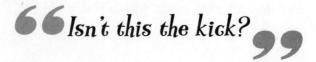

*Isn't this the kick?*

She started to crack up as she looked at the rose-colored gown again.

From his perch on the stool, Jonah looked from Kiyoko to the dress and back again. "You find it amusing?"

Kiyoko doubled over.

Jonah's brows shot up. "For the love of God, share," he ordered her.

"I truly don't know where to start, except to tell you that Charlanne Papel is in the house, and she has tattooed a copy of herself as Kali Goddess of Destruction onto the entire front of her very tall body. It will show through that sexy little number."

"What?" Jonah slid off his stool.

"I just saw her. She's early, and Belle sent me to warn you." She covered her mouth to stifle her laughter. "I think Belle's going to see if it's real."

"You're not exaggerating?" Jonah asked, growing pale.

"When have I been known to do that?" Kiyoko demanded, grievously insulted.

"Where's Demetria?" Jonah asked Liv.

"She's in a meeting and I'm not to disturb her," Liv answered.

"Oh, little one, for this she *must* be disturbed," he said, whipping a cell phone out of his trouser pocket.

"Belle's calling her," Kiyoko assured him.

> **Kiyoko put four and four together and figured this was the meeting Olivia had not been allowed to attend. Which bit the big one, frankly.**

He nodded and punched a button. "Demetria, have you talked to Belle? Yes, a full-body tattoo. That's what I've heard, too." Then he listened.

He disconnected, put the phone in his pocket, and crossed to the assistant. He took the dress from her, his hands moving with lightning speed as he slid a muslin bag over it, lifted it off the hanger, and draped it like a dead body over the assistant's arms.

He said, "Take it into the off-the-rack room. Stat."

Watching her scurry away, he made another call, this one to Ms. Bishop—who, it turned out, had just been debriefed by Demetria.

And who, it turned out, was sitting next to Gianna Russo, the designer of Charlanne Papel's dress. Kiyoko put four and four together and figured this was the meeting Olivia had not been allowed to attend. Which bit the big one, frankly.

Then Belle called. *She* was with Charlanne, and they were on their way.

Jonah turned to Liv and Kiyoko and said, "Move away from the door, girls. This could get ugly."

Kiyoko grabbed Liv's wrist and dragged her behind Jonah.

They waited, staring at the doorway. Kiyoko said to Liv, "She must be under a lot of stress. People under stress do very strange things. I read about a man who started eating his office furniture."

Liv shrugged. "I read when I'm stressed."

"Why am I not surprised?" Kiyoko asked.

Just then, Ms. Bishop, her assistant Delia, Demetria and her assistant Dwayne, and Lynn Stein walked en masse into the room. Dwayne was carrying a sketchbook. Also with them was a woman with sad brown eyes and big coffee-colored lips, whom Kiyoko assumed was Gianna Russo.

Kiyoko noted the absence of Alexa. That meant that *no* interns had been at the meeting—a fact that she hoped was not lost on Liv.

Jonah said, "Ladies, a pleasure."

Dwayne shot him daggers.

"Not so much," Demetria said. She wagged her cell phone at him. "Belle sent us a picture. I just forwarded it to you."

Jonah looked down at his cell phone.

"Oh," he said, moaning.

He showed it to Kiyoko and Liv. It was a shot of Belle posing with Charlanne Papel. The full-body tat was practically glowing.

"Oh my God!" Liv cried. "That is positively revolting."

"What did I tell you?" Kiyoko said. She squinted at Jonah. "And you accused me of exaggerating!"

"We have a plan," Demetria announced. "We're going to tell Charlanne that the dress was held up. Then we'll present her with a new Russo creation, and ask her if she would consent to wearing that instead."

Dwayne turned the sketchbook up and showed them a brill gown made of twisted pieces of fabric and jeweled metallic strings running diagonally across the torso. The arms were encased in more of the same, and the faceless figure wearing it looked like a samurai and a geisha at the same time. It was the coolest dress Kiyoko had ever seen.

"God, I love this dress just as much," Kiyoko blurted, violating the no-speaking-by-interns edict. "It's smashing."

Gianna said, *"Grazie."* She admired her own work, head tilted, arms folded. "It's so different. Not my usual style at all. It's opening up a new world for me."

Delia pressed her earpiece against her head and said to Bishop, "They're on their way."

"And in return . . ." Gianna said to Bishop, with a self-satisfied smile on her face.

Top Diva cleared her throat and said, "Lily will wear another design by Gianna in the show."

Kiyoko gaped. This was earthshattering. Lily was one of the most supermegafamous fashion models in the world. With two dresses in the show, both worn by celebs, Gianna Russo had pretty much taken over the entire *soiree*.

"Lily? What about the dress we already planned for Lily to wear?" Jonah asked.

"There are other models," Bishop said dismissively.

"How did you manage that?" Kiyoko blurted, then shut her mouth and look abashed. She said through clenched teeth, "Sorry. Remaining silent."

Gianna laughed as Bishop said, "You may know that Kiyoko is the younger sister of Miko Katsuda. I understand she and Lily are good friends."

"Flying in together. Miko's in the show, too," Kiyoko said. She was angling for Miko to get a Russo dress, too.

"Equally impetuous," Gianna said. She smiled at Kiyoko. "And charming."

*"Douzo yoroshiku onegaishimasu,"* Kiyoko said humbly, bowing. It was the formal Japanese way of saying "nice to meet you" and she was hoping it would get her off the hook for yakking out of turn and promoting Miko.

Gianna bowed back as if she had been to Tokyo two thousand times as the head of a hugely influential fashion design house.

"So that's the bargain," Gianna said to the group. "I allow you to 'lose' one of the most fantastic dresses I have ever designed, and in return, I get *two* dresses in your show, one worn by Lily."

"Yes," Bishop said.

So no go for Miko. Well, no one could fault Kiyoko for trying. Except for Top Diva. She could fire her, actually.

Still, Gianna Russo was certainly leveraging the lemons into lemonade. Kiyoko thought maybe she should ask Gianna Russo for advice on her musical career.

Jonah meaningfully cleared his throat as Charlanne, Belle, and Charlanne's people swept into The Closet.

"Charlanne," Bishop said, spreading open her arms. "You're here."

Charlanne melted into Bishop's embrace. Kiyoko was agog. She had never seen anyone *touch* Bishop before. She had begun to suspect she was a computerized hologram.

"I have some sad news and some fabulous news," Bishop continued smoothly, gently pulling away.

Charlanne lifted her brows. Kiyoko had yet to hear her speak and she was very interested in doing so. Charlanne sang in an ultra-soprano range, and Kiyoko wanted to know if that that was her natural voice.

Belle gestured to Kiyoko and Olivia to leave with her. Kiyoko was extremely bummed. She wanted to see how this played out.

When they got out into the hall, Belle said to them,

"The fewer witnesses the better, in case she does decide to throw a tantrum or, even worse, her cell phone."

Kiyoko said, "What if Charlanne asks Gianna Russo to recreate the original dress? It's the one she approved."

"Gianna will tell her there's no more fabric," Belle said mournfully, then rolled her eyes. "And that she can't get the beading done in time. She, Bishop, and Demetria have a million excuses lined up."

"What happened to her?" Kiyoko asked. "Does she have a brain tumor?"

"Sssh," Belle said, chuckling as she put her finger to her lips. She said in a whisper, "I asked her why the tat. She's in love."

Kiyoko scratched her head. "With who, Count Dracula?"

"No." Belle waited a beat. Her eyes were shining. "With Johnny Tortomakto."

"That cannot be true," Liv said as Kiyoko made a strangled retching sound and covered her mouth. Johnny Tortomakto was a totally crazy, younger version of Ozzy Osbourne in his wilder days. "He bites chicken heads off during his concerts!"

"Only in Europe and Asia," Belle drawled. "The U.S. Humane Society got on his case so he had to stop."

"But she's a pop star," Kiyoko argued. "She's all fluffy and friendly and . . ."

"And now she has a big weird tattoo," Belle said. "Let this be a lesson to you girls. Don't ever permanently disfigure yourself to impress a guy."

"Writing it down, chief." Kiyoko pantomimed typing on a keyboard.

"Listen, I need you to go do those errands," Belle told her. "Charlanne Papel isn't really our problem. She's Fashion's problem." She gave Liv a wink. "And your boss is torqued out about the whole thing."

"I'll go," Kiyoko said. She turned to Liv. "*Hasta la vista*, baby."

ⓖ     ⓖ     ⓖ     ⓖ

After Kiyoko hustled off, Liv and Belle stood together in the hall. Belle snickered and shook her head. "I never had to handle these kinds of situations when I was freelancing. I just reported 'em. It's very interesting being on the management side."

*I wonder if Belle knows that* interesting *is a Winnie-the-Pooh word,* Liv thought, as she glanced in the direction of The Closet, wishing she had been allowed to stay.

"Surely she knows how inappropriate her tattoo is," Liv said. She remembered the beginning of summer, when she and her loftmates had gotten henna tattoos, only to discover after the fact that Bishop abhorred "body art."

"C'mon, girly girl. You know the drill. When you get to a certain level of celebrity, you don't worry about being inappropriate," Belle drawled. "That's part of the allure of celebrities—they're above all the bourgeois concerns of the middle class. But that tattoo is so out of character for her. It's so frickin' ugly."

They both burst into giggles.

Belle grabbed Liv's arm and dragged her farther down the hall, out of earshot, into the bathroom. They dissolved into helpless laughter. Liv laughed and laughed, holding her stomach as the sheer delight of the tension release overcame her. She just couldn't stop.

"Okay, we really need to settle down," Belle said.

They took a few moments. Then Belle pushed on the door and the two went back into the hall. Charlanne and her people, Bishop, Gianna Russo, and Demetria were walking toward them. Charlanne and Bishop were walking arm in arm, and Charlanne was singing in French in her signature beyond-soprano voice.

Belle surveyed the scene. Charlanne stopped singing and said, "Belle, drinks at eleven tonight? My suite?"

"I'll bring the cigars," Belle said, and the two women laughed as if at a private joke. Then Belle smiled at everyone. "I've got some things I need to deal with." With that, she trotted off.

"Liv," Demetria said, gesturing for her to join the

group. Surprised by the warmth in her tone, Liv scooted beside her.

The group sailed down the hallway toward Bishop's office. Bishop said to Charlanne, "I'll have the sketches of the new dress faxed to your stylist."

*"C'est bon.* Then she and I will get to work on my makeup and hair," Charlanne said, with a wave of her hand.

She, Gianna, and Bishop moved on ahead, leaving Demetria and Liv walking a bit behind them.

Demetria said in a low voice to Liv, "She's going with the new design, in red silk and silver tissue."

"Oh." Liv brightened. "I have some earrings I just did with rubies and silver wire. They'd look smashing." She smiled shyly. "At least, *I* think so. But if I—"

Demetria's features hardened. Startled, Liv stopped in mid sentence.

"Every item in this show is the result of hours of negotiations for product placement," Demetria informed her. "We don't just toss in a pair of earrings at the last moment."

"Oh." Liv blinked. She knew that wasn't precisely true. There were still a lot of slots deliberately left open so that Bishop could dispense them as she pleased.

"I—I didn't mean to presume," she said.

"Well, you did presume. Bishop and I decide what's in the show, and what's not."

Demetria turned and walked a few steps away. Then she turned back.

"You have filing to do now, I believe."

"I'll get right on it," Liv said, swallowing back tears. She stared at Demetria's retreating back. There it was: Demetria's payback for the times Bishop had slighted her in favor of the daughter of her rich and powerful friends, the Bourne-Cecils.

Feeling as though she'd been slapped, Liv returned to the mail cart. She was about to retrieve her jumble of folders when a young guy with close-cropped hair stepped out of the cubicle beside it and jabbed a finger first at her and then at the cart.

"*You,*" he said. "Listen, my mail cart is not the city dump, got it?"

"I'm so sorry," Liv said, hastily gathering up her folders. "It won't happen again."

"You got *that* right," he snapped.

As he watched, she carried the folders into her cubicle and sat down in her computer chair.

*I will not cry,* she ordered herself. And she didn't. But just barely.

## chapter six

"**T**his is cold," the angry restaurant patron told Mel. It was the third time the thin-faced, hook-nosed woman had called Mel over. First there was ice in her water glass. She didn't like ice. Then she didn't want salted butter with her bread.

"Um, it's gazpacho," Mel replied. "It's traditionally served cold. On the menu it says—"

"I want it heated."

"All right," Mel said, picking up the bowl of gazpacho. "I'll take care of that right away."

As she turned to go, the woman said, "And bring me some more bread. And butter. *Un*salted."

"Right away," Mel said again.

As she carried the bowl to the noisy, busy kitchen, she indulged herself in a little fantasy in which she dumped the bowl of gazpacho over the woman's head. Next, a very hot guy would sweep through the restaurant, inform Mel (in front of Ms. Gazpacho Head) that she had won the National Book Award, and whisk her off in a limo to life among the literati.

And then she said to Miguel, "My customer wants her gazpacho heated."

> **As she carried the bowl to the noisy, busy kitchen, she indulged herself in a little fantasy in which she dumped the bowl of gazpacho over the woman's head.**

He stared at her. "It's gazpacho. It's served cold."

"I told her that."

He sighed. "Did you tell her that before she ordered it?"

"No," Mel said. "It said it on the menu."

"You should have made sure she knew," he informed her. "Some people don't read menus very carefully."

"Oh," she said. "Well, okay."

He took the bowl from her. Her mouth opened, closed, opened again . . . and she had no idea what she wanted to say to him.

He said, "Your other order's up. Table twelve."

She walked to the counter where the finished orders were lined up, found her three veggie burgers, and started trying to arrange them against her forearm and wrist, the way she had seen waitresses do back in the innocent days when her only restaurant experience was eating in them.

But the white china plates were very heavy, and she was afraid she'd wind up dropping them. *Liv didn't mention how tough Miguel was,* Mel thought. *And how demoralizing being a waitress is.*

She settled for picking up two plates and carrying them through the swinging double doors that led into the dining room. Table eleven, table . . .

*Oh my God.*

The hostess at table thirteen was seating Jack and four people Mel didn't know. One of her tables.

She took a breath and brought the two veggie burgers to twelve. She said to the diner who hadn't yet gotten his burger, "I'll be right back." Then she hung a very sharp U.

"Yo! Mel!" Jack called, rising out of his chair.

Mel hurried back into the kitchen. She retrieved veggie burger number three, remembered that such a thing as trays existed, and loaded a brown tray with the plate and three iced teas. Her hands were a little shaky. What was he doing here?

She delivered the burger and the iced teas and walked over to Jack's table. He rose and showed her a piece of paper.

"This fell out of your backpack when you were walking away," he said.

It was her half of her W-4 for Moe's. With the restaurant's address carefully printed in Mel's handwriting.

"Listen . . ." He glanced at the others and moved

away from the table. "I'm sorry," he said, lowering his head. "I dissed your internship, and that *was* pompous. It's just . . ." He gave his head a shake. "No 'just.' None. I *just* can't shut up, can I?"

There was a beat where no one spoke. Then she relented and said, "Okay. Thanks."

He looked around at her workplace—which, while not exactly a dive, was close. "Couldn't they just pick up your expenses?"

"Don't go there," she suggested. "Ever." She gestured to the table. "Are these your friends?"

He smiled and said, "This is my writing group. We've been meeting at this Hawaiian place but they told us we were too loud. We met at a writing seminar two summers ago."

"And you've been together ever since?" Mel asked, impressed.

"Yeah. Can I introduce you?"

She nodded, and they walked back to the table. He said, "Everybody, this is a writer friend of mine"—he gave her a questioning look—"from school. That's Haley, Tamara, Thom, and Schliemann."

"Hey," Mel said. They all smiled at her.

"Mel's interning at *Flirt*." He said it like he was really proud of her.

"Wow." Tamara's eyes lit up. "*Flirt* is the *Vogue* of our times."

"Maybe you'd like to join us sometime," Jack said. "We read our work to each other once a week."

"You probably know that Jack placed for a Preslim Award," the skinny guy named Schliemann informed her grandly.

"Oh." She didn't actually know what a Preslim Award was, but it sounded impressive. By the modest-but-proud smile on Jack's face, she assumed it *was* impressive.

"We give ourselves assignments, too," Haley added. "We're reading from *The Norton Anthology of Short Fiction*. We read a story and discuss it. We're doing 'The Moths' this week."

"Jack's been going on all the way over here about your work," Thom told her. "He says you're a genius."

That was cool to hear, especially after their conversation about *Flirt*. He had pretty much come right out and said that she was a moron.

"You really should join us sometime," Haley invited her.

"Well, that would be nice, but I'm kind of busy most of the time," Mel replied apologetically, which was true. She held up her order pad. "Speaking of which, I'd better do my job. Let me get you some menus."

Miguel was standing in front of the double doors to the kitchen, his arms folded over his chest, watching her as she arrived to place their orders.

"Friends of yours?" he asked.

"They're a writing group," she replied, aware that she wasn't exactly answering his question.

"I hope they're an eating group," he said.

She showed him their order. "One of them ordered gazpacho. I told her it was cold."

"Good," he grumped.

*Sheesh,* Mel thought.

ⓖ     ⓖ     ⓖ     ⓖ

Alexa had just sent a check-in e-mail to Manuela when Lynn IMed her to come to her office. She scooted away from her desk and trotted down the hall to Lynn's office, which was wall-to-wall fashion photography and black-and-white lacquer furniture. There were two Starbucks cups and a half-eaten sandwich positioned at the corner of Lynn's desk. An enormous computer monitor took up the rest of the desk, and Lynn was hunkered forward, moving a mouse with her left hand while she sipped from a third Starbucks cup.

As Alexa knocked on the door jamb, she craned her neck so she could see the monitor. It contained the last shot Alexa had taken of Sister Pauline before she fell off the wall.

"Alexa, come in," Lynn said, swiveling her head to smile at her intern. "The nun pictures are great. We're using one in the fashion show. Give me her release so I can scan it in."

"Oh." Alexa grimaced as she entered Lynn's office. She'd been so relieved to have the card back that she'd forgotten why she lost her camera in the first place.

Now she semi-tucked in her chin and nervously studied the floor. "I forgot to tell you. *Siento*, but my school principal said we can't use them." She looked up at Lynn through her lashes.

Lynn's lips parted as she blinked in disbelief. "*What?* Why not?"

Alexa swallowed hard. "Well, because they're nuns and it's not permitted."

Lynn's frown grew; she pushed back from her desk and crossed her arms. "Alexa, I just spent the last hour manipulating half a dozen images of her. Why did you take pictures of her if we can't use them?"

"I'm so sorry," Alexa said. "I didn't know. I . . . I should have told you right away. I was so nervous about the card."

"The card that wasn't damaged at all," Lynn said, cocking her head as she ticked her gaze from the monitor to Alexa and back again.

"I know. It's . . . I'm so happy about that," Alexa said miserably.

"But now I can't use the pictures I want off it," Lynn said, drumming her fingers on her keyboard.

"Not the policeman with the puppy?" Alexa said. "I thought you would love that one."

"It's a cliché." She sipped her Starbucks. "We call them BLS's—Big Lug Shots."

"Oh." Alexa wilted.

"Well, that's frustrating about the nun pictures," Lynn said. "Maybe you can talk to them. We could make a donation or something." Lynn cricked her neck and moved her shoulders. "Maybe I should talk to them. Or Bishop."

Alexa jerked with massive alarm. If Mother Michael found out that *Flirt* had these pictures, she would know that someone had snuck into the closet and taken the memory card.

*No. I can tell Mother Michael I took the card out just before I fell. She will have no way to prove otherwise.*

*Oh my God, will I have to actually lie to a nun?*

"Mother Michael told me it was an invasion of Sister Pauline's privacy," Alexa said. "I got in huge trouble for doing it."

"Well, hell," Lynn said. She took another sip of Starbucks. Her computer pinged, signaling the arrival of e-mail from the in-house *Flirt* system. "You should have told me."

"*Siento,*" Alexa said again. "*De veras,* Lynn." Her English was beginning to desert her. Too much adrenaline was coursing through her body, and she was getting jittery.

"All right. Let me think about what to do." Lynn set down her Starbucks cup. "You're officially off the clock for tonight."

Alexa tried not to let her relief show.

"We're going to be shooting a lot of layouts tomorrow, and I want you to start looking for celebrities on the street. No shooting them inside the building or within a block of our doors. Beyond that, they're fair game. Got it?"

"*Sí,*" Alexa said, warming at the thought. What fun that would be. Like pranking, only with permission.

More e-mail came in on Lynn's computer. Ping-ping-ping; they were piling up. Alexa didn't know how Lynn kept everything straight, but she did.

"Go on home," Lynn said. "I'll be starting down in Bryant Park tomorrow. Meet me there."

"I will," Alexa said. "Good night, Lynn."

"Night," Lynn said, her attention back on her monitor. "Okay, Trey, what do you want?" she murmured to herself.

◉    ◉    ◉    ◉

**"*What fun that would be. Like pranking, only with permission.***"**

Alexa took the subway home and entered the building, nodding at George, the night doorman. She took the elevator up and went into the loft. It was quiet. No one appeared to be home.

She went up the stairs into her room, preparing to do her homework, when she caught sight of herself in the full-length mirror. There was a strange white spot on the hem of her skirt. She slipped it off and examined it. There were three of them.

"*Ay, Dios,*" she said. They were pigeon droppings!

This was a problem: Her parents had limited her to one school uniform for the first month—they were that uncertain that she would be able to keep from getting kicked out. Luckily, she was able to wear her own white blouses, but the plaid skirt was the only one she had. She couldn't go to school tomorrow with pigeon poop on her skirt. She'd already washed it last night, to get out the mud from her fall. Was she going to have to wash it every single night?

She took off her uniform and put on a pair of black sweats and her *Gaucho* sweatshirt. She slipped into flip-flops, picked up the loft's stainless steel laundry basket, gathered a few more dark clothes to wash, and grabbed her chemistry textbook. With the laundry basket on her hip, she headed back into the elevator.

As she had hoped, the small laundry room was deserted. There was a table for sorting and a green plastic

> **66** *As he bent to check his clothes, Alexa couldn't help an admiring glance at his butt.* **99**

chair beside the dryer. She set down the laundry basket, loaded the washer, grabbed her book, and plopped down in the chair. The light was a bit dim to read by, but she flipped open her book with a determined sigh.

"Oh, sorry," said a voice in the doorway.

She looked up. A very cute guy carrying a jute laundry basket stood at the entrance to the room. He had on dark gray workout shorts over nice tanned legs, a white sleeveless T-shirt, and sandals. He had a reddish-brown goatee and close-shaven hair.

*Ay, que guapo.*

"I have some things in the dryer," he said, over the noise of the washing machine. He put his laundry basket beside Alexa's on the table. She scooted the chair over against the wall so he could open the dryer door. As he bent to check his clothes, Alexa couldn't help an admiring glance at his butt. She doubted that Lynn would say a pic of *that* was cliché.

The man frowned and said, "They're still damp. Huh." He looked at her with dark brown eyes that reminded her of El Torero's. Since he was bent over and she was sitting down, they were pretty much at eye level, and Alexa's pulse quickened.

"Does it always take this long?" he asked her.

"It's usually pretty quick, I think."

"Well, it's not tonight." He shut the door and turned the dryer back on.

She could smell his scent—spicy, with a note of sunscreen—and she smiled. "Are you new in the building?"

"Staying with a friend. 4A. You?"

"I've been here since June," she said.

"NYU student?" he asked, leaning against the dryer. He crossed his legs at the ankle and fanned himself with his hand. It was moist and warm in the laundry room. Alexa hadn't noticed until he'd shown up.

*He's flirting with me,* she realized. She had just broken up with Ben and wasn't looking for a new boyfriend just yet. Ben had been funny and cute but just too clingy. But this guy was *handsome.* Like in a grown-up way.

She said, "No, I'm an intern. At *Flirt.* Do you know it?"

"Fashion magazine, right?" When she nodded, he said, "You must be busy. All they talk about on the news is Fashion Week. I guess that's a pretty big deal."

*Talk about an understatement.*

"It's huge," she told him. "Hundreds of shows. Twenty minutes each." She snapped her fingers one-two-three. "All the big designers have shows, at Bryant Park and at other venues in the city."

"I see," he said.

"*Flirt*'s putting on a fashion show with people from all over the world," she said. "A lot of famous people, too. *And* we still have to work on the magazine."

"Wow." He quirked a brow. "It must be intense."

"Lots to do," she agreed.

"I don't know much about fashion," he admitted. "Most of the time I don't get it. The models wear weird clothes that I never see in the stores. And the way they walk . . ." Standing in place, he mimicked the hard stomp and hip thrust of models walking down the runway, and she laughed.

"And they're so diva," he added.

*"De veras,"* she said. "True. Oh god, there is this one . . . we have to switch dresses because . . ." She trailed off, realizing she wasn't at liberty to discuss it.

"Because she got fat?" He leaned toward her and said conspiratorially, "I guess if you gain an ounce you're in big trouble."

She giggled.

"Not too fat," she said mysteriously.

"Pregnant?" he asked.

She laughed, mildly shocked. "No! If you must know, she got a tattoo. A lot of models have them. But this one is very big." She made a little face as she visualized it. "It was so crazy-*loca* of her to do that to herself. And now she has to wear a different dress, and we pretended to lose the first one, and the designer gets to have an extra dress in the show because of it." She gave her head a determined shake. "I can't tell you any more than that."

He wrinkled his nicely tanned forehead.

"Hey, no fair. This is juicy stuff. Much more interesting than what I'm doing." He raised his brows up and down. "What's the tattoo like?"

*"Horrible,"* she said, gesturing to herself. "All over the place. She looks like a monster." Then she realized she really should shut up. She looked back down at her book.

"You were reading," he translated. "Sorry."

He turned and opened the dryer, reaching in and feeling around. He said, "Oh, good," and grabbed his basket. He piled in jeans, more T-shirts, socks. Guy clothes. They smelled fresh.

He picked up the basket. "Well, it was nice meeting you." He laughed. "Actually, we haven't met, have we? I'm Shane Morris."

*What a nice name.* "Alexa," she said. "Alexa Veron."

"From . . . ?"

"Argentina," she said.

*"Mucho gusto."* He inclined his head.

She grinned. "Do you speak Spanish?"

"Just enough to get in trouble." Was that a wink?

She couldn't tell. "Maybe we could get in trouble together sometime." He grinned at her. "Maybe after Fashion Week?"

"That sounds . . . *posible*," she said, feeling sassy and flirtatious.

"Cool," he said, his grin getting bigger. "Well, *buenas noches*."

"*Lo mismo*." She watched him go, getting another view of his cute behind. After Fashion Week, yes.

Then the washer went off and she checked her skirt before she put everything in the dryer. No more pigeon caca. She transferred the load and started the dryer. She thought about going back upstairs to study, but she had found a nice little hidey-hole and now that Shane—*I like that name!*—was gone, she could burrow in and do some studying.

The hum soothed her as she went back to her chem book.

Bases, acids . . . salts. She yawned and felt her eyes drifting shut.

*I'll check the dryer again in a few minutes,* she promised herself.

⊙     ⊙     ⊙     ⊙

Seated at table thirteen, Jack and his friends discussed the meaning of the short story "The Moths" for half an hour. Mel hadn't read it, but after listening to snippets of their conversation while she buzzed around her tables, she wanted to. These guys knew their stuff. They were well-read and they knew how to talk about literature. It was exciting.

Finally, her shift was over. Her first four hours on the job were now history. She walked to Jack's table and said, "I'm going now. The other waitress is named Lisa, and she'll be waiting on you."

"We should go, too," Jack said.

The writing group started breaking up, putting away their notebooks and papers. They worked out the check, and then Jack carried the bill to the cashier while Mel went to the employee's break room to grab her backpack.

She took a quick glance in the bathroom mirror— unfortunately, she looked slagged—and went back into the dining room as Jack and the others headed for the front door.

"Walk you home?" he asked, slowing for her.

*Cool.*

"Okay," she said. "We walk."

Everyone went out the front door, into the warm night. The others drifted away, calling good night, telling her it was nice to meet her, leaving Jack and her alone as they walked down Broadway.

Jack gestured to her backpack. "Hey, let me take that."

"I've got it," she said, although the truth was, her back was very tired and sore. Her feet were aching. She wondered if she would get used to the grueling routine of waitressing.

Jack was also surprisingly quiet as they headed toward her loft. She'd looked forward to a rousing discussion, but nothing happened—at least on a verbal level. Nonverbally, she was having all kinds of reactions to his nearness. They had some chemistry going, that was for sure.

One more block, and they reached her building. She stopped outside the green metal door and said, "We're not allowed to have guys in."

He took a step toward her. She tingled. Was he going to kiss her? Would she kiss him back?

Then he reached up and brushed a strand of hair away from her face as he opened her door for her.

"Good night, Mel," he said. His voice was hushed.

"Good night, Jack." Her own voice was husky; she was whispering like he was.

66 *She was having all kinds of reactions to his nearness. They had some chemistry going, that was for sure.* 99

Then the Smile spread across his mouth, and twenty thousand volts zinged right through her. It was unbelievable, what that smile did to her nervous system.

She watched him go as she entered the building. George was at his command console; he waved at her and she at him. She took the elevator up and went into the loft.

Gen and Charlotte were curled up on the couch with schoolbooks. The TV was on, and Gen was listening to an iPod. They looked up and Charlotte smiled at Mel. Gen kept listening to her music.

"How did it go?" Charlotte asked.

"My feet are dead," Mel admitted. "My back hurts."

"I'm sorry," Charlotte said feelingly. "Maybe you should take a bath."

Mel reached behind herself and patted her backpack. "I have too much to do."

She left them and went upstairs to the room she shared with Gen. She set her backpack down and booted up her laptop.

**From:** bishop@flirt.com
**To:** melanie_h@flirt.com
**Subject:** Script
Send me the next attempt of the script by eight A.M.
—JB

No please, no thank you. That was Bishop. Setting all thoughts of her homework on hold, Mel groaned as she pulled out the script that Jack had ridiculed. She began to read it over.

*A sassy and chic filigree of a sandal.*

She opened up the script file she'd e-mailed herself and compared it to Bishop's copy, yawning as she looked it over, wincing at each slash and exclamation point Bishop had scrawled in the margins. In Bishop's parlance, exclamation marks meant *give me a break.*

Mel yawned again. To the list of words starting with "trite and timid," she could add "tired."

Rather than reading the script, she stared at the many, many corrections; they blurred and stretched until it seemed that all her script consisted of were things that needed fixing.

Without really thinking about what she was doing, she Googled the short story "The Moths" and read about a third of it. It was astonishing, a piece written in Hispanic dialect about a young girl dealing with the death of her *abuelita*, her grandmother. Mel wondered if Alexa knew about this author. Alexa wasn't much of a reader. But this was incredible.

*If I could write like that . . .*

She went back to "The Moths" soaking up the words, the wonderful words.

Then she shook her head and went back to work.

*A sassy and chic . . .*

She hit Delete.

It was nearly eight o'clock . . . and time to start over. Ms. Bishop was right: What she had written was trite and timid. She had read it all a million times before, in her pre-internship days, even though the only times she looked at fashion magazines were at a friend's house, or when she went with her mom for a pedicure.

She thought some more about "The Moths." About the power of the words. The boldness.

*That's what I need*, she thought.

She let herself finish "The Moths." Then she sat quietly and really let herself *feel* its power. Words like this were why she wanted to become a writer.

*If I can put that sense of power into my script,* she thought, *I'll really have something.*

Taking a breath, she started writing.

## chapter seven

**T**he dinner party was just beginning when Liv arrived at Bishop's town house on the Upper West Side. Gwyneth Paltrow and Catherine Zeta-Jones were there, Catherine chatting up Trey Narkisian.

Demetria was *not* there, and Liv wondered if she had been invited. Liv would have assumed an invitation from Bishop to a party at her home was tantamount to a command performance for the head of the Fashion department.

Ducking into her rooms, Liv hastily changed into a sleek black Dolce & Gabbana, redid her makeup, and made sure her hair was in place. Then she layered on some of the jewelry she had made—tiny, abstract swirls of black opals at her ears, equally tiny swirls around her neck. They sparkled on slender wires like planets in the cosmos, and Liv smiled at her reflection. She was onto something here.

> **"** *Liv would have assumed an invitation from Bishop to a party at her home was tantamount to a command performance for the head of the Fashion department.* **"**

She joined the party, asking the bartender at the black marble bar for a glass of cranberry juice and seltzer. There were at most twenty people, the powerful celebrities working the room with ease. Liv had been to a hundred parties like this—perhaps a thousand—with her parents, who were one short rung down from royalty in the U.K., and true royalty in the art world.

Sipping her juice, she caught her breath as she spotted James&Jane, whom she had not noticed at her first sweep of the party. That was how they were called—James&Jane—and they were revered in the fashion world not only for their innovative designs, but for their huge influence in the arts. One could detect dashes of their Dali-like style in the new opera sets for *Carmen* at the Met. They'd consulted with Cirque du Soleil. They had partnered with Issey Miyake. They were *everywhere*.

For some, their private antics overshadowed their genius—they were wont to have very public rows that on occasion included broken dishes—but it was a potent reminder of Jo Bishop's enormous stature in the fashion world that they were here.

As Liv gazed at them, Jane turned her head and looked back at her. The pale Englishwoman with a buzz cut and three or four sets of eyelashes had on a peach-colored Gianna Russo blouse similar to the rose-colored gown originally designed for Charlanne Papel.

Jane tugged on the sleeve of James, who was faced

away from Jane. The bald man tilted his head, then gazed in the direction Jane indicated—directly at Liv.

James brightened, and they both came toward her, moving slowly, like panthers. James was wearing a sleek peach silk shirt and gray trousers, and he looked like his wife's twin.

They drew near, and he smiled more broadly at Liv. Jane's smile was nearly identical.

"Bourne-Cecil, is it?" he said.

"Yes," Liv said breathlessly.

"Charmed," he said, air-kissing her.

She did the same. "The pleasure is mine," she replied, her manners rescuing her as her legs turned to jelly.

"Interning with Jo-Jo?" Jane said.

"Yes," Liv replied.

"She's a taskmaster," Jane said.

"But you'll learn from one of the best," Jane concluded.

Liv took a breath, wondering if it would be rude to mention her own work. In America, one pushed oneself—"tooted one's own horn"—but in England, that was considered to be quite vulgar. It didn't come naturally to her. Besides, James&Jane were British, like her, and she was afraid they would find her brash.

However, they *were* the same couple who fought in public.

"I'm also doing some designing, as well," she told them.

James cocked a brow, looking rather devilish. "Oh? Doing things up for Jo?"

"Not exactly," she hedged. "I've had some of my things in a couple of articles." She winced at how obnoxious that sounded. "Earrings in *Flirt* and *Jolie*."

"Oh. *Jewelry*," Jane said delightedly. She reached out a hand toward Liv's earring. "We love the shinies, don't we, James? Did you design these? They're brilliant."

"Thank you. Yes, I did." Liv could feel herself blushing as she bit off the words that would deflect the compliment—*They're nothing, really. Just some things I whipped up.*

"So you designed them?" James queried. "For whom?"

"I don't really have a 'whom.' So far, it's just me. I have so much to learn."

"Those are wickedly brilliant," Jane opined. "You've grasped the need for tension in the work."

"Tension," Liv repeated.

"Why, yes," Jane said. She gestured to Liv's earring.

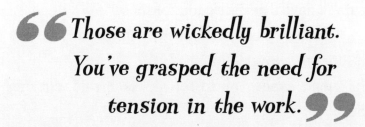

**❝ Those are wickedly brilliant. You've grasped the need for tension in the work. ❞**

"Just as with, well, anything, one needs a conflict. You've got the swirling bits, but the asymmetry poses a threat to the integrity of the composition. That's juicy, luv."

Liv was astonished. "You see that in my work?"

"Indeed." Jane smiled at the earring, and then at Liv.

"May I show you a couple of other things?" Liv asked. "Get your thoughts on them, if it wouldn't be too much of an inconvenience?"

"It wouldn't be inconvenient at all," James assured her grandly. "We love nurturing talent, don't we, darling?" He put his arm around his wife's waist.

"Indeed," Jane said, leaning her head against his cheek.

Liv rushed into her bedroom and retrieved the antique jet beaded loops from the wooden chest she kept her finished pieces in. Then, on impulse, she grabbed the ruby set she had tried to tell Demetria about.

She returned to the main dining room and held both pairs out to Jane. The designer clapped her hands, seized one of the ruby earrings, and said, "*These*. Splendid. Stunners." She took the other one and held them against her ears. "I have a perfect outfit for these."

"Oh, then please, take them," Olivia said. "As my thanks for our conversation."

"Don't expect me to refuse," Jane said, cocking a brow.

"Please. They're yours," Liv said.

⟲    ⟲    ⟲    ⟲

Kiyoko hightailed it down to Central Park West, to the luxe building where Donato dwelled like a hunky faboo gargoyle in the penthouse. She flashed her *Flirt* badge to the doorman, also whipping off the top of the cardboard gift box for his inspection, to reveal the nougaty goodness ensconced inside.

After phoning up, he allowed her into the marble-and-possibly-gold elevator and she was whisked into the stratosphere like little Sailor Moon herself.

She popped out directly across from another marble door. Since it was the only one, she figured Donato's assistant was lurking behind it, awaiting her summons.

But before she could find the bell, Donato himself opened the door! He was wearing his black leather pants and a black T-shirt, and he said to Kiyoko, *"Noite boa."*

*"Você fala o português!"* she cried. *You speak Portuguese!* Even cooler, he remembered that Kiyoko did.

She showed him the box and said, "I brought your Italian candies. From Belle."

**❝ She was whisked into the strato-sphere like little Sailor Moon herself. ❞**

*"Grazie."* Zzzap! The world-famous Donato smile shot through her like ten thousand volts. "Come in, *mulher bonita.*"

He was calling her a beautiful woman! He was *flirting* with her. Not that this was a new thing. Most guys—correction, all guys—with whom Kiyoko came into contact wanted her on some level. She had incredible animal magnetism. But for God's sake, Donato was practically the inventor of animal magnetism.

She bopped on into a world of black leather furniture, black marble floors, and gray walls. There were stacks of CDs everywhere. And an acoustic guitar. His guitar! And cobalt-blue bottles of mineral water and chocolates—what kind? Ritter Sport—oh, so much glorious input!

She said, "Do you like your place? Do you need more water? Are we doing enough for you?"

He raised a brow. "You're quite the live wire, aren't you? Is that how they say it in English?"

"Yup," she replied exuberantly. As he took the box from her, she said boldly, "I'm a musician, too, you know. My partner and I are providing the music for Yuko Sato's fashion show."

"Forgive me," he continued, as he put the candy down on his coffee table, "but I have no idea who Yuko Sato is."

Kiyoko snorted. "Only one of the most famous

fashion designers in the world." She grinned at him. "We work with Matsumoto and Kanno. They're huge in anime," she added helpfully.

"I'm so ignorant," he said, grinning back. "But I congratulate you on your achievement."

Then his phone rang. He checked his watch and said, "Ah. That's Italy. I have to take it."

She knew that was her cue to leave. She turned to go, saying, "Enjoy the sweets."

*"Grazie,"* he replied. "Maybe next time bring me a CD of your music, okay?"

*Oh. God.* It was not a joke, right? He meant it? *Donato* wanted to hear her music?

She turned back around to assess his sincerity factor. But he was in the process of whipping out his phone from his tight black leather pants, his lion's mane shielding his face, so she said, "Sure thing!" and let herself out the door.

She collapsed with her back against the cool marble, her heart booming like a big *taiko* drum, when her own cell phone went off.

She whipped it out and checked caller ID. It was Cody, texting.

**DJCody: We're coming tomorrow!**
**KIYoKO!!! You said Thursday!**
**DJCody: And yet!**

**KIYoKO!!!: Plan?**

**DJCody: Nobu at 7 PM? You can?**

**KIYoKO!!!: I'll try!**

**DJCody: Just do it!**

**KIYoKO!!!: OK, Nike–Yoda!**

**DJCody: Gottago!**

Kiyoko let out a whoop, then covered her mouth because what if Donato heard her? Then she called Belle and reported the successful delivery of the candy.

"Good. Keep going," Belle said, referring to the Kiko-Do list.

"I'm a goer!" Kiyoko told her.

⊙　　⊙　　⊙　　⊙

*From the Journal of Melanie Henderson*
*Tuesday, September 12*
*Maybe I have lost it. My fourth attempt at the fashion show script is worse than the others. It's midnight and I just reread the story I wrote for class. Those guys were right. The ending isn't there. Nothing's there. I'm completely losing my confidence.*

So as not to wake Gen, Melanie was writing in her journal on the sofa in the main space of the loft when she heard someone coming down the hall from the Lyrics'

> ## Her heart skipped a beat and her cheeks went hot.

quarters. She took a breath and looked up.

Her heart skipped a beat and her cheeks went hot.

It was Nick, in his usual painter's pants and a sleeveless white T-shirt. He saw her and gestured toward the kitchen.

"My mom made some sun tea today," he said. "Herbal, as in non-caffeinated. I mention this because from the looks of it, you can't sleep."

Mel closed her journal. Beneath her dark blue Japanese-style robe, she was wearing a pair of navy blue drawstring shorts and an olive *Nature Conservancy* T-shirt—modest enough for tea with mixed company at midnight—even though that mixed company was a guy she was still seriously crushing on.

*I almost forgot how much I like you,* she thought, feeling conflicted. The memory of Jack hovered behind her like her own shadow. Maybe Nick was too complicated. Maybe she should start over . . . with someone else.

But . . . this was *Nick*. The sexy painter of incredible visions; the patient, wise listener; the masculine presence in a loft filled with women. Jack was exciting and edgy . . . and a high school student. Nick was grown up.

She rose from the couch and followed him into the kitchen. She got two glasses from the cabinet while he retrieved the tea from the fridge. She filled the glasses with ice from the icemaker—crushed ice for her, ice cubes for him. She knew many of his likes and dislikes. She knew a lot about him.

She just didn't know how he felt about her.

*Jack is nothing, nothing, nothing. Just a guy at school.*

*Who writes. Who reads the great short stories of world literature for a non-credit extracurricular writing group.*

"Why can't you sleep?" he asked her as he poured the tea and handed a glass to her. "When you came home from work, you looked dead on your feet."

*Oh?* She hadn't known he'd even seen her.

"Bishop," she said, taking the glass from him. Their fingers brushed.

He nodded with the look of one who had been there, done that. His mom had worked at *Flirt*, and he had watched a lot of interns come and go through the summers. He knew how demanding Josephine Bishop was. "What does she want you to do?" He sipped his tea.

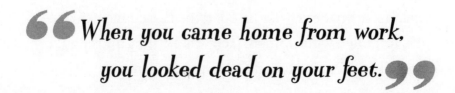

66 **When you came home from work, you looked dead on your feet.** 99

"Write the script for the fashion show," she told him.

He looked taken aback. "That's nuts," he said. "All those shows are scripted by professionals. Firms shell out the big bucks for them. If they even have a narrated show. Don't most of them just let 'er rip? The music goes on, the models parade, and we all go home convinced we need forty thousand dollars worth of new clothes."

"You sound like Jack," she said, before she realized what she was saying.

"And he is?" Nick asked. His voice was neutral.

"A boy at school. He says I'm selling out. That I have all this *talent*." She said it like it was a dirty word, and she huffed with exasperation as she heard herself. "Never mind. I've settled this with myself. I'm learning tons at *Flirt*. I'm not being ruined."

"Mel, you're just tired," he replied. "You *have* made peace with this." He cocked his head. "What exactly did he say to you that rattled your cage?"

Something about his tone gave her pause. He really wanted to know. Was he jealous? What if he was? They both knew he was still getting over Anastasia.

*I wish you were really ugly,* she thought. *And a jerk.*

"I read a story in class," she told him, leaning back against the counter. Her shoulders were aching. "That I wrote, I mean. A couple of people in my workshop thought it was confusing—well actually, everyone did, except for him. But he loved it."

Nick grinned lazily at her.

"No, he really did," she said. "He's blunt. Bishop-blunt. He went *on* about how great it was. Then he found my fashion show script and he started making fun of it."

"You know that a lot of people don't get the fashion industry. Including you, granola girl. But if I may?" He raised a finger from around his glass. "This is the same script Bishop is having you do and redo?"

She nodded. "It's all wrong."

"Which means?" he pressed.

"I'm all wrong. As a writer." She heaved a sigh. "Maybe I've lost it."

He cocked his head, gazing at her. She felt self-conscious, but she also liked his attention. She liked him.

*Okay, I'm glad you're not an ugly jerk.*

"This is the problem with being in the arts," he said. "We struggle to pull our visions out of ourselves, and then we look to other people to see if they're any good. But what if they're wrong?"

She processed that. "What are you saying? That

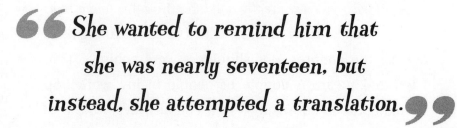

**She wanted to remind him that she was nearly seventeen, but instead, she attempted a translation.**

no one has the right to judge our work?"

"I'm saying that it's hard to find your own voice," he said. "Look at you, Melanie Henderson. You're only sixteen, and you're in a magnet school for creative writing, *and* working directly under Jo Bishop."

She wanted to remind him that she was nearly seventeen, but instead, she attempted a translation. "I'm too hard on myself?"

"Yes, Mel, you are. Way too hard on yourself," he said. "This should be a fun year for you. But you're already tied up in knots."

"You've got that right," she said, wincing as she tried to straighten her sore, tired back.

"Here." He set down his tea and came over to her. "Turn around."

Mel closed her eyes as Nick rubbed her shoulders. His hands caught up bits of her robe and she half-feared, half-hoped that he would suggest she remove it so he could massage her through the single layer of her T-shirt. But he didn't, only kneaded her shoulders and upper back. It was exciting and awkward at the same time. His fingers were very skilled. She knew he was an excellent kisser.

She knew she wanted him to turn her around right now and kiss her again. She could still feel their first kiss, preserved for all time in her body memories and her memory-memories. The Kiss of Nick.

"What's wrong?" he asked her in his silky, gentle way.

She closed her eyes as waves of lusty-like roared through her. *Keep going,* she begged those fingers.

She blurted, "I'm afraid Bishop will send me home. She said some really mean things to me."

He exhaled. She felt his breath against the nape of her neck.

"What does Kiyoko call her? Top Diva? That's really a perfect name for her."

"She's a genius," Mel said reluctantly. "Not Kiyoko. Well, I mean, Kiyoko is probably a genius, but Bishop is who I mean."

"She's a *survivor,*" Nick corrected her. Knead, knead, knead. "Think of what it takes to survive in the fashion world. The tenacity. The drive." He tapped her shoulder as he stepped away.

*No!*

"Maybe you could take a page from *her* journal. She does it, and then she moves on. No angst, no regrets."

She turned back around and looked at him, wondering if her face was red and sweaty. "All I am is angst."

"Jo Bishop has weathered a lot of storms," he said. "Before you got here, you probably had a pretty serene life, am I right?"

She nodded.

"Storms are new," he said. "But you've got the stuff to get through them, Mel." His voice grew soft. "That's my way of saying that yes, you are way too hard on yourself."

"Thank you," she said, her voice barely above a whisper. She was loving this conversation.

"Now, I have a very important question to ask you." He waited a beat. She took a slow, deep breath, preparing herself for a shift in the wind.

Then he said, "How are you guys set for toilet paper? I have to make a run to the store in the morning."

She burst out laughing. She smashed her hands over her mouth so she wouldn't wake up the whole house, but she couldn't stop. It felt so great to laugh that she kept laughing some more. It was infectious; Nick joined in, covering his mouth, too, until they just stood there vibrating.

"I think we're good," she said, and for some reason that set them both off again.

## chapter eight

"**A**lexa!" Emma Lyric cried from the doorway of the laundry room. As Alexa bolted awake, Emma whipped out her cell phone and shouted into it. "She's here! I found her! She's okay!"

"What . . . ?" Alexa grabbed Emma's cell phone from her hand. *Nine A.M.?* That couldn't be right. It was just after dinner when she had come down here . . .

"Did you sleep down here all night?" Emma asked her, giving her a tight hug. "We've been looking for you all over town! The police are upstairs. We called your parents and—"

The horrible truth slowly dawned on Alexa.

"*Sí*," she cried. "I did! I slept down here all night! Oh my God, Emma, I'm late for school!"

"Oh, Alexa," Emma said, laughing weakly. "We're just so glad you're safe." Then she scowled as she studied the angle of the chair and light, taking a few steps backward and peering into the room. "I sent Gen down here and she said she didn't see you. Maybe it was too dark."

"Please, I have to get to school right away," Alexa begged. She threw open the dryer and pulled out her skirt. She started to take off her sweats when she realized that her blouse and everything else she would need were still back upstairs at the loft.

"Oh, Emma, please, call me a taxi," she pleaded as she gathered everything into the stainless steel basket. "Call my school principal."

"We will. Upstairs," Emma said. "I can't get any reception here."

"Dios mio," Alexa murmured.

"Don't worry. It's not the end of the world," Emma comforted her.

⊙      ⊙      ⊙      ⊙

But it *was* the end of the world.

And being late was the least of Alexa's problems.

In all her black-and-white penguin glory, Mother Michael stood beside the open closet door while Alexa stared into it in horror. Her mind raced almost as fast as her heartbeat. What could she say? What *should* she say?

For behold: The bin where Mother Michael had placed Alexa's camera was lying tipped on its side on the floor. Her camera was nowhere to be seen. It had been *stolen*.

"So you came in here at some point, went into the closet without permission, and took your camera. Also without permission."

"No, Mother," Alexa assured her. "I did not. You keep the door locked, no?"

Mother Michael's eyes ticked to the pencil can. Alexa caught her breath. If she asked her about the key, Alexa wasn't sure she could lie to her.

"Then can you tell me who did take it?" the nun demanded, crossing her arms and glaring down at Alexa as only a good Catholic sister could do. "Because all evidence points to you, Alexa. Who else would do such a thing?"

*Mary Beth?* Alexa wondered. *But why? To get me in trouble?*

Alexa hung her head. This didn't add up. Why would Mary Beth give her the card and then take the camera? Unless . . .

*Chrissie?*

"Alexa Veron, answer me," Mother Michael snapped.

"I—I don't know, Mother," Alexa replied, which was the truth. She lifted her head. "It seems that a thief broke in, and took things."

"No. Not *things*. One thing. Your camera," the principal said.

Tears welled. She had been late, her homework unfinished, her camera gone . . . and now this.

"I want it back," Mother Michael said. "Today is Wednesday. By the end of school on Friday, that camera

> ## "That camera had better be on my desk. Or we will have to discuss the possibility that St. Catherine's is not the place for you."

had better be on my desk. Or we will have to discuss the possibility that St. Catherine's is not the place for you."

"Mother," Alexa gasped. She couldn't get kicked out! Her parents would have her back on a plane within twenty-four hours. The *Flirt* show was Saturday night!

"How am I supposed to get it back, if I didn't take it?"

"That remains to be seen," Mother Michael said. "You may go." She glanced at the plain black wall clock over the transom, then back down at Alexa. "How good of you to join us for *lunch*."

Apparently Emma's note stating that Alexa was late because she had not been feeling well did nothing to appease Mother Michael. Alexa wanted to explain, but she didn't think it would be a good idea to tell Mother Michael that the real reason she was late was because the police had detained her to ask her a few questions about her whereabouts last night. It seemed that not everyone believed she had slept all night sitting up in the laundry room—especially after Gen Bishop had sworn she had checked, and Alexa had not been there.

*No one believes me about anything I say.*

Of course, Emma'd had to inform Bishop about the incident. If Bishop *also* heard about Mother Michael's ultimatum, she might kick Alexa out before her parents did.

"You may go," Mother Michael said.

"Yes, Mother," Alexa murmured, turning and trudging out of the room.

She walked to the beautiful dining room, inhaling the mingled odors of cooked food. She hadn't eaten any breakfast, and she knew she should be hungry. But she didn't feel like eating.

The students in their white blouses and plaid skirts were seated at long tables. Mary Beth saw her, half-rose, and waved. Beside her, Chrissie was examining the food on her white plate. She looked up, met Alexa's gaze, and did not smile.

*Why not smile at me? We are the three Amigas Pranksteristas!*

Unless . . . *Chrissie* had taken the camera.

*But why?* Alexa thought. *Chrissie would have no reason to get me in trouble.*

"Hi," she said to them both. Mary Beth grinned at her and stuck her elbow out, indicating the empty place on her right.

"Saved you a seat," Mary Beth said. "Missed you this morning. What was it today? Did you get busted for taking pictures of Mother Michael?"

"No, but I was in her office," Alexa said, gazing at Chrissie. But Chrissie's head was down; she was pulling apart a piece of bread.

"Not again! Why?" Mary Beth asked.

"Someone unlocked the closet and stole my camera," she said, still looking at Chrissie's head.

"No way." Mary Beth dropped her fork. The noise startled Chrissie, who jerked up her chin. She met Alexa's gaze, and her cheeks turned pink.

"Mother Michael thinks I did it," Alexa continued, studying Chrissie's face. She looked guilty. "She wants me to return it by Friday."

"Or . . what?" Chrissie asked, looking back down at the fragments of bread on her plate.

"Let's talk about it later," Alexa said, her alarm bells ringing. "I'm hungry. Are they still serving?"

"Yes," Mary Beth said. She got up and followed Alexa as she turned and walked to the serving line.

"I swear, I didn't take it when I got the memory card," Mary Beth said in a low voice. "How did she know it was gone?"

"The door was open."

"That's so *amateur*. Who would be so careless?"

Alexa debated. Then she said, "Mary Beth, do you think Chrissie might have taken it? For a joke?"

"*What?*" Mary Beth's lips parted. She was clearly astonished. "Why would she?"

> **" But she had a feeling that by mentioning it she had set something in motion, and it was too late to stop it. "**

"I don't know," Alexa said. "Maybe she's jealous? She doesn't want to share you?"

"Oh, please. How old are we?" Mary Beth reached for a fork, knife, and spoon and clattered them on Alexa's tray. "Alexa, I can't believe you're accusing her."

Alexa squirmed. "I'm sorry. It's just . . . no one else but you two and I knew it was in there. And it was the only thing taken. And Chrissie knew there was a spare key in the pencil can."

Mary Beth ran her fingers through her hair. She looked in Chrissie's direction and said, "Chrissie's been my friend since ninth grade."

Alexa murmured, "Never mind." But she had a feeling that by mentioning it she had set something in motion, and it was too late to stop it.

ᔕ  ᔕ  ᔕ  ᔕ

*I'm not looking for him,* Mel told herself, as she scanned the main hallway of her new school for Jack. The kids at PS 99 looked pretty much like the kids at her school in Berkeley—same street fashions, same haircuts, same backpacks. But she suddenly felt like she was at sea in a little boat. Homesickness rushed over her in waves.

*What am I doing here?* she wondered. *I should go home. I'll never make it here in New York. It's just too different.*

And then she saw him.

He stopped and turned almost as if she had spoken his name aloud. There was a glint in his eye and he broke into a happy smile as he acknowledged her and trotted up to her.

Her tension eased. Jack was like an anchor—someone she knew. Relaxing a little, she stifled a yawn.

"Hey, Mel," he said softly. He reached down and brushed her hair out of her eyes again. "You need to take it easy."

His concern both frightened and soothed her. She didn't want to have a schedule that made people worry about her. Before she could say anything, he went on.

"I was thinking about something. Stop me if you think it's a bad idea, but what about writing a story together?"

It wasn't at all what she was expecting him to say. In fact, she didn't know what she *did* think he was going to say.

"I don't know," she replied. "I've never written with anybody."

"It'd be good," he said, looking eager. "California meets Jersey."

"Oh? You're not from New York?" she asked.

"With this accent? Are you kidding? People say I sound like Tony Soprano." He laughed. "C'mon, let's just give it a try. I'm thinking that if you have to write a story a week by yourself, you'll burn out."

She considered.

"Just one story," he said. "If it doesn't work out, you haven't lost anything."

"Except maybe an A on my story," she jibed.

"Ms. Kaneshige grades for effort," he said. "If she sees you working hard at your craft, she gives you a good grade. Cs are for slackers."

It would be nice to work with him, listen to his thoughts about writing. Hear about the stories he had read.

"Okay," she said. "Let's do it."

"Great," he said, and his blue eyes practically glowed. "I'll e-mail you tonight."

"Okay."

"Can't wait." He whirled around and trotted away.

She watched him with a smile on her face. And then she, too, hustled off to class.

ⓖ     ⓖ     ⓖ     ⓖ

*Freedom!* And a new policy, handed down by Bishop: Despite Saturday's looming fashion show, the interns were to have three solid hours a day to work on their homework. Then they could help their mentors for three hours and three hours only. After the show . . . who knew? Bishop wasn't saying. But the Flirtistas, as Alexa had begun calling them, figured the place would pick back up.

It was certainly picking up for Kiyoko. She had done all her overdue homework during French, then done tonight's homework in one hour, and was now creating all kinds of superb tunes in manga psychedelic that would blow Donato away. Cody's plane was landing this afternoon and the plan was to meet up at Nobu at seven. Then they would go to M/K's studio and get their music done!

Kiyoko hoped Nobu at seven worked for Belle. Her mentor, who still thought Kiyoko had no homework and that the three-hour-edict therefore did not apply, had told her that she didn't care how she arranged her time, as long as she pitched in and fought the good fight against the never-ending demands of the rich and famous.

Today's agenda included babysitting the children of Ice Daddy, the famous rapper, who was going to sing "Yo Mama Do" in the fashion show while twenty outfits by fringe designers from all over the world went down the runway. The craziest of the batch had to be a sort of animal pelt "construction" by a designer from Norway.

The monstrosity was like that old Björk swan dress,

only it was a sort of a cross between an elk and a fish, if such a thing could be imagined. Anti-fur Mel had gone out of her mind when she'd seen pix of it on the *Flirt* website, which was showing a little bit of the fashion show here and a little bit there, tantalizing fashion mavens and press agents alike.

Their girl from PETA was down on the sofa now, still working on that script for Bishop. At this point, Kiyoko thought the writing of the script had devolved into cruel and unusual punishment. She wondered if it was some kind of Zen test of Mel's mettle or something. Because why was an intern writing the script, anyway?

No time to ponder that now. Kiyoko had a date with twin boys named Maurice and Uledi. She grabbed up her laptop, her BlackBerry, her Treo, her iPod, and her canister purse, which was crammed full of half-eaten bars of Toblerone, a Metrocard, a hairbrush, and her book of *Shonen Jump* anime characters. Surely that would amuse her young charges—while *she* worked on Project Donato.

Then she threw caution—or rather, dollars—to the wind and cabbed it over to Ice Daddy's beautiful penthouse at the W. The W! Where Yuko Sato and her daughter Mariko were staying this very night!

She grinned to herself as a willowy woman in a shimmery gold pantsuit let her in. She was Ice Daddy's wife, and the mother of Maurice and Uledi.

The twins were three, with big brown eyes and chubby cheeks. Kiyoko imagined herself as a mother, all good humor and fun games, and she told Madame Daddy not to worry about her children because she, Kiyoko Katsuda, had a black belt in babysitting.

But the lady wasn't listening. She was gathering up a lot of makeup and cramming it into a tiny gold purse.

"I'll be back in a couple hours," she said, as she bolted for the door. "My cell phone number is on the refrigerator."

"Okay, I need to leave by six thirty," Kiyoko called after her.

But she had lost her at "Okay."

Kiyoko settled in, determined to be brill. She squatted on her heels and hung her hands between her knees, saying to the little boys, "Right, then, lads, what would you like to do?"

Maurice burst into tears.

Uledi threw up.

⊙　　⊙　　⊙　　⊙

Dressed down in black walking shorts and a white cotton T-shirt, Liv was alone with Demetria in The Closet. Jonah warned them not to mess up his organizational system, and then he had left to go to a party. Demetria had some sushi and Japanese pickles sent up, and they had eyeballed the collection while they ate. Or rather, while Demetria ate and Olivia nibbled. She was far too excited to actually eat.

After days of spinning her wheels, she was finally getting a chance to work the show. Clothes were pouring in from all over the world. There were mounds of sheer evening dresses, chunky sweaters, and slingback kitten shoes. There were frilly skirts and pencil skirts, palazzo pants (not over?) and a black nightgown so sensual that Liv was actually a little embarrassed to touch it.

As she observed, Demetria began to make sense of the chaos. It was quite stunning to watch her mind at work, pulling this blouse with those pants, adding a chain belt, taking away a scarf. The clothes were like the syllables of a language Demetria spoke, but Liv didn't. She was a bit humbled. Demetria might treat her poorly on occasion—well, on most occasions—but she certainly could teach Liv a lot.

"Now, watch what I'm doing here," Demetria said, as she picked up three bright sweaters and carried them over to one of several racks she had arranged in a circle. Dresses in various shades of red and orange hung on the next rack over. On the one next to that, coats in purple, green, and blue. Then six meltingly exquisite white evening gowns. And on around the circle.

"I'm thinking a kaleidoscope," Demetria said, eating the last piece of sushi. "The models shift and move and the colors form and reform. Do you see it?"

Liv slowly walked around the circle. She did!

"You can build around anything, but the point is, you have to build something," Demetria said, walking to the sink and washing her hands thoroughly. "You can't just cram a bunch of clothes onto a stage and call it a collection."

"Right," Liv murmured. She already had so many questions—exactly how *did* one build a collection? How did Demetria have the nerve to mix and match the way she did?—but Liv didn't want to break the spell. She and Demetria were getting on as never before.

"Okay, we have our base. The clothes themselves. Now let's add the fun." Demetria's eyes gleamed. "The little pieces of glass in the kaleidoscope."

Against the wall farthest from the door, boxes and boxes sat on shelves, all marked with the names of the companies that had sent them. Dior, Tiffany & Co., Obafemi, Kim, Magnusen. Demetria dipped into one box and pulled out a tiny purse covered in black rhinestones and shaped like a leaf.

"You think evening wear, right?" Demetria said, grinning as she dangled it from the hook of her finger. "But I think, leaves are green in nature. So I take it to a sky blue coat."

It worked. Liv didn't understand how Demetria knew it, but it looked perfect with the coat.

Then Liv got it. She said, "Tension. Asymmetry."

"Yes." Demetria blinked. "Exactly. Very good, Liv."

Liv was so happy. Finally, they were getting along. Finally, she saw a glimmer of respect in Demetria's eyes.

*Thank you, James&Jane,* she thought feelingly.

Demetria walked over to the bins and said, "Let's see what else we can do. Oh, here's James&Jane's contribution. Jonah e'ed when it was couriered over this afternoon. I'm sure it will be something wonderful. Oh, it *is*."

She reached into the bin and pulled out a pair of earrings.

A very familiar pair of earrings.

Liv's ruby earrings, in fact.

"Huh," Demetria murmured.

Liv's heart pounded. Was Demetria remembering Liv's description of her earrings, putting two and two together? Was she going to whirl around and demand an explanation?

*May I have an explanation, too?* Liv thought.

"These are really lovely," Demetria said. She held one up to her ear and peered in the mirror. "You know, they might go well with the new gown Gianna Russo is designing for Charlanne."

Liv couldn't believe it. Had Demetria completely forgotten about their discussion? Had she heard a single word Liv had said when she had been describing them?

*What on earth should I say if she asks me for my opinion? Should I confess?*

*Confess to what? That James&Jane are passing off my work as theirs?*

Liv's heart pounded as Demetria put them back into the bin and picked it up, saying, "I'm going to take some pictures of these and e them to Charlanne's stylist."

Demetria started walking out of The Closet. Liv trailed after her, freaking out in silence.

"I'll just take a couple of shots," Demetria said as they went into her office. There were several photographs of Demetria herself, from her glory days as a supermodel. She was still very beautiful and glamorous.

She set the earrings down on her desk and pulled a digital camera out of one of the drawers. "I've got some black velvet somewhere," she murmured, looking through the drawers. "Here we go."

She spread the velvet on her desk. Then she sent Liv to get a floodlight and some gels. She arranged them with as much ease as Lynn Stein. Then she shot the pictures.

"The craftsmanship is excellent," Demetria mused, as she shot away. "Take a look when I'm finished."

Liv murmured, "Mmm." *This is so incredibly awkward. I need to talk to James&Jane. As soon as possible.*

## chapter nine

**M**aurice was screaming. Uledi was no longer vomiting because there was nothing left in his little body to throw up. Kiyoko's clothes were *infected* and she was more than a little furious with Mrs. Daddy. It was eight P.M. and she had not answered any of Kiyoko's six calls.

*And* Kiyoko had not had any time to work on the music.

*This is horrid*, she thought. *This completely bites.*

**DJCody: DOKO NI?**
**KIYoKO!!!: Still at Ice Daddy! No one is coming home!**
**DJCody: Hurry!**

She hung up and stared at her two little charges, whom she had imprisoned in their gated area. One could not properly call it a playpen. But she had thrown all their toys into it in an attempt to keep them occupied. Uledi had thrown up on most of them, too.

Kiyoko debated calling Belle. She didn't want to be a whiner, but she had been on the clock more than the allotted three hours. Belle was off entertaining divas and she was watching their children. Kiyoko was sure Belle would tell her it was the price of admission.

Then the door crashed open and Ice Daddy's woman blasted on in. *Blasted* being an important word.

"Hey there!" she slurred happily. There were several beautiful people with her. Everyone was glammed up, made up, and free of throw up, unlike Kiyoko.

"How did it go?" she asked Kiyoko. Then her eyes swept downward and she said, "Oh, *crap.* Why didn't you call me?"

"I did," Kiyoko said. She pointed to the refrigerator.

Mrs. Daddy staggered over to the fridge. She blinked at the number and then she started to laugh. "Oh my God! I wrote the number down wrong!"

*What a scream,* Kiyoko thought.

She staggered back to Kiyoko. "Oh, you poor, poor girl! Look at you! Smell you!"

"Oh, it's all right," Kiyoko said unenthusiastically. "I just have a date next."

"No!" Mrs. Daddy cried, covering her mouth with her perfect manicure. "Oh, we have to fix you up!" She grabbed Kiyoko's hand. "Come with me. I have *tons* of clothes. It's Fashion Week! Everyone's got lots of clothes!" She waved at her people, three of whom were female. "Come with us and let's fix up Yukiko!"

"Kiyoko," Kiyoko said, as the other women

> ## "We are going to fix you up so your man won't be able to remember his own name!"

crowded around her and swept her down the hall. "What about your twins?"

"José!" Mrs. Daddy called over her shoulder at some tall bloke who was not Mr. Daddy. "Take the babies, all right?"

Then she smiled at Kiyoko. "We are going to fix you up so your man won't be able to remember his own name!"

❧     ❧     ❧     ❧

Liv stood and waved to James&Jane as they appeared in a whirl of attention at the roped-off check-in area of Donna Summer, a club devoted to the steady and wearying predecessor of house music known as disco. They had returned her cell phone call with a text message suggesting they meet here "for drinks." As Liv was well under the legal drinking age in America, she had already bought herself a cranberry juice and seltzer, her standard non-alcoholic drink.

James&Jane were both clad in black silk and crimson nail polish, carrying the metro thing to the hilt,

Liv thought, as Jane swerved around James to get to Liv first.

"Darling," she said, giving her double air kisses on her cheeks. "So lovely of you to call us."

"Hello, my beauty," James said next, with more kisses.

"Thank you for coming," Liv replied.

They all sat down, Jane on the opposite side of the booth, so close to the edge that part of her extremely small butt was hanging off the seat. She sat there until James, standing in the aisle, gazed down at her and cleared his throat. She huffed and scooted over, so that he could sit down, too.

A waiter arrived. James&Jane both ordered martinis and rattled off a dazzling array of starters. Liv's brows shot up. Had they not eaten for the last . . . month?

"Darling, did you hear?" Jane said. "We sent in your earrings to the show!" She flashed her white teeth at Liv. "What a funny little caper, eh?"

James's forehead wrinkled. "We did *what*?"

"Yes! I knew they deserved their place in the sun and I knew Jo-Jo had to take whatever we sent, so . . . !" Jane clapped her hands together and then splayed them open, like a magician doing a card trick.

"Not again!" James shouted at his wife. "You thieving cow!" He buried his face in his hands, then stared through his fingers at Liv. "Don't believe her. She's a . . . a kleptomaniac. She keeps stealing people's work and *I have had it, Jane!*"

People started staring at them.

"Oh, God," Liv murmured, completely at a loss for what to do. "Um, oh, please . . ."

Jane turned on him. "I did not steal them! She gave me the earrings, and I was going to let Jo-Jo know after the show—"

"You liar! You are crazy!" James jumped to his feet with his martini in his hand. It sloshed everywhere as he gesticulated. "Oh, God, Bourne-Cecil, forgive us. She's just over the top." He shook his martini glass at Jane. "I can't go on with you, you . . . you poseur!"

People started murmuring.

"Poseur? Everyone knows I'm the force behind J&J, you working-class twit!" she flung back at him.

James rolled his eyes. "She comes off as a toff, doesn't she? But guess what . . . she's *Tasmanian.*" His voice was shaking, and his upper-class English accent was crumbling into Cockney. "You're a right Tasmanian devil!"

He turned on his heel and walked toward the exit. Jane knocked over her drink as she followed after him, leaving Liv to stop it from dribbling into her lap with the club's useless but trendy polyester napkins.

*What just happened?* she thought, her hands shaking. *What on earth did I just witness?*

Nobu. 8:39.

Wearing more makeup than Shiseido sold in a year to all the women in Tokyo, Kiyoko walked in with a pair of gold heels slung over her shoulder, along with the bag for her laptop.

Cody leaped from the table and dashed to her side. He looked just as she had pictured him, except that he was wearing gray dress pants and a cool white shirt with the sleeves rolled up his forearms. He still had brown hair and dark lovely eyes in a face with a square jaw and a bit of bristle. Still had a body made for modeling in a life-drawing class.

He gave her a big hug and said happily, "My God, what happened to you?"

"It's a bit much, isn't it?" she said. She was wearing a gold tulle bubble skirt, a black satin corset, and the combat boots she had worn over to the Daddys' penthouse. She said, "I yanked the shoes off in the cab. Wrong size."

Cody squeezed her again and said, "You look great. In an unusual way. As usual." He kissed her cheek. No lip action, she noted.

"Matsumoto and Kanno are really jet-lagged." He waved at their table. The tall director sported his trademark lion's mane of stark white hair; the diminutive composer wore a black braid down his back and a Yomiuri Giants baseball cap. They were both wearing chichi Italian-cut suits.

"There's Mariko Sato. Her mom was too tired to come."

"Then she was in the W at the same time I was," Kiyoko mused, as a really, really pretty Japanese girl dressed in a clinging silk cream-colored boatneck top and a pearl choker looked up from drinking a frothy beverage in a martini glass and smiled.

At Cody.

At Kiyoko, she practically shot out her claws and hissed.

*So it's like that, eh?* Kiyoko thought, as she made a show of looping arms with Cody and kissing his cheek. He looked pleasantly surprised. They had not been romantic before he had left for Japan. She had been in someone-else's-girlfriend mode. Now Matteo was gone.

And Mariko was . . . not happy to see competition. Kiyoko wished she had worn the high heels of death after all.

"Listen," she said. "We may have some business, but we have to move fast. It's *Donato*, Cody! He wants a CD from us."

"Get out," he said. "You are kidding, right?"

"No." She waggled her brows. "So as soon as we're done here, let's go to the studio and get to work." She patted her laptop bag. "I started on some stuff for him."

"Great. Okay." He grinned at her. "You've got the touch, Kiko."

> "You've got the touch, Kiko."

She was really glad she had agreed to peace in their time.

As they approached the table, Matsumoto and Kanno both rose and bowed. Kiyoko bowed back, more deeply, since she was the junior partner and a mere female to boot.

"It's so nice to see you," Kanno said in English. They would all have to speak it because they had a *gaijin*—foreigner, i.e., Cody—in their midst.

"You also, Kanno-san," Kiyoko said.

"Katsuda-san, what a pleasure," Matsumoto added, inclining his head.

"You flatter me, Matsumoto-san," Kiyoko said, falling into the manners of her native land.

Mariko had not gotten up. It was incredibly rude. But she did hoist her drink, and said in totally fabulous American English, "I'd get up, but I'm just dead."

*Maybe not yet,* Kiyoko thought. *But it can be arranged.*

"I'm Kiyoko Katsuda," Kiyoko said. "Cody's music partner."

"About that. You will be receiving a credit for the Sato music," Matsumoto said to Kiyoko.

"Oh, that is too generous," Kiyoko said politely,

thinking privately, *Heads will roll if I don't get credit.*

Kiyoko took a seat beside Matsumoto—since Cody had not saved her a seat beside *him*—and thought about all the small talk she did not want to indulge in. There was music business to discuss!

But something told her not to discuss it in front of Mariko. Thus, she was hamstrung.

"I suggest we order dinner, and then we can catch up," Kanno said.

The waiter glided over as if he had psychic powers. Kanno did the ordering in Japanese—meat and vegetables cooked over hot rocks—and then poured Kiyoko a cup of sake. She tipped it back like a sailor and let it slide down her throat.

Mariko leaned toward Cody and poured him a cup. Kiyoko could smell her perfume all the way from where she was sitting.

They chatted about the flight from Japan, and the weather in New York, and then they got down to Fashion Week. Mariko poured Cody more sake. Kiyoko slugged more back as well.

Her cell phone vibrated in her purse. She reached inside and pulled it out, checking the faceplate for the caller.

*Olivia?*

She'd have to take it later. She slipped it back in her purse and listened attentively to Mariko, who was bragging about her mother's cool collection.

"We rented the Tent," she said proudly. The capital-T Tent was the largest of the four tents erected at Bryant Park, which was on Sixth Avenue. It was an all-black space featuring a central or U-shaped runway. Its total capacity was 1,250 spectators, and it cost forty-two thousand dollars to rent for a show. Kiyoko knew all these facts because Bishop had forced all the interns to memorize them.

"We're in the Promenade," Kiyoko said. It only cost thirty-six thousand dollars and housed one thousand spectators. "We needed an all-white space."

"Ah, well, that will be nice," Mariko said dismissively. She simpered at Cody and put her hand on his arm. "Would you please pass me the edamame?"

Kiyoko watched the action as she tried to decide what variety of jealousy she was experiencing—the jealousy of a good friend and music partner who had not yet had a chance to talk with same? Or a proto-girlfriend, held at bay by . . . same?

Realizing that alcohol was dangerous in a situation like this, Kiyoko decided to switch to tea. She was beginning to get her dander up and she needed to show restraint. Evidently, Mariko did not share her concern—another frothy drink showed up in front of her, and she drank it down as if it were Calpico.

Then the food came. Everyone cooked their paper-thin slices of excellent meat on the hot rocks, which were installed beneath take-away sections of lacquered tabletop. Each diner had a pair of long chopsticks, and as each delectable morsel was cooked to perfection, one simply popped it into one's mouth.

Kiyoko covertly watched Cody as Mariko showed him how to do it. She laughed when he dropped his first piece onto the rocks, and deftly retrieved it and put it on his plate.

Mariko had another drink.

The phone buzzed again. Olivia again. Kiyoko was flummoxed.

"Excuse me," she said, bowing to the table. She picked up her purse like a football and clomped in her combat boots to the bathroom. One glance at herself in the mirror confirmed that she looked like Olive Oyl. She had yet to see Mariko's feet, but she doubted she was wearing steel-toed kickers from Carnaby Street in London.

She pulled out the phone and speed-dialed Liv.

"Kiyoko?" Olivia's voice was blanketed in disco noise.

"Yes. Where the hell are you?" Kiyoko asked.

"Oh, my God, it's a mess," Olivia said. "I met with James&Jane to discuss my earrings. They ordered up loads of snacks. Then they had a terrible row and left. And I've got to pay the bill."

Kiyoko waited for the punch line.

"My parents insisted that I not spend so much

time in clubs and things, now that I'm in school," Olivia continued. "And when they see the bill, which they will see, since they pay it . . . oh my God, Kiyoko! James&Jane are completely insane, both of them!"

Kiyoko parsed. *That* was the real issue, the insanity of them.

"Tell me," she urged Olivia, "exactly what happened."

"They just . . . she stole my earrings, and he said she does it all the time, and—"

Just then Mariko swayed into the bathroom. She shot Kiyoko a glare worthy of a Kabuki drama and crossed her arms over her chest.

"Olivia, listen, I'm out with Cody," Kiyoko said, giving her chin a little lift. "Can I call you back in a few?"

"Oh, it's all right, Kiyoko. I'll just use my card and sort it out later."

"I'll text you in a bit," Kiyoko promised.

"Please, give him my best," Olivia said, and rang off.

Kiyoko put her phone in her purse. In Japanese, she said, "Fancy meeting you here." Or the equivalent thereof. Despite being Japanese, she was far more comfortable with Portuguese.

Mariko said, "Cody said you two are friends."

"We are. Wonderful, close, fantastic friends," Kiyoko assured her. She turned her back on Mariko to check her makeup in the mirror. Ye gads, there certainly was a lot of it.

Mariko said, "He said you were *just* friends."

Kiyoko felt a bit of ice frost around her heart. She honestly didn't know what to say. Was that true? Did she want it to be true?

She turned around. They faced off like gunslingers until Kiyoko said, "Cody is my music partner."

"He did all the music for my mother without you. I think it's wrong to give you credit."

"Lucky thing you aren't my music partner," Kiyoko said.

She started to go. Mariko moved into her way. Kiyoko looked her up and down and thought, *I could take her.*

She smelled alcohol on Mariko's breath and said, "Please, Genkai"—that was the name of a famous anime warrior girl—"take it easy."

Then she skirted around her and back into the dining room, to find that the three men were getting ready to leave.

"We've called cabs for you," Kanno said to Kiyoko. "We're very tired, and we need to work with Sato-san tomorrow to rehearse for the show."

"Oh." Kiyoko looked at Cody. He mimicked typing on a keyboard, and she nodded. They'd work online. No problem.

*"Donato,"* she whispered, as she reached up on her tiptoes and brushed his lips with hers.

*He kissed her back!*

"Online," he said, his voice a little breathy and excited.

*Maybe it* is *love,* she thought.

*"Daijoubu,"* she said merrily.

⟲    ⟲    ⟲    ⟲

Alexa was whirling in circles when Kiyoko blew into the loft from the elevator. Gen and Charlotte were sitting on the couch giggling. Mel was upstairs doing homework.

"I took pictures you cannot believe today!" Alexa cried. "I saw Paris Hilton! Cameron Diaz! Halle Berry! And . . ." She stopped spinning. "El Torero!"

"Shut up!" Kiyoko shouted, jumping up and down. "Shut up, shut up, shut up!"

*"De veras*, I did!" she cried.

Then, even though Alexa knew the Katsudas were not big on hugging, she hugged Kiyoko. Snapping El Torero had been on her eternal list of Things to Do Before I Die.

"Let's see the pix," Kiyoko demanded, "before I get to work on my own work."

That slowed Alexa down. "I can't," she admitted. "I had to use a camera from *Flirt* and Lynn made me turn it in before I came home."

"Well, I'm sure they're brill," Kiyoko said. "Now, listen to me, angels, Olivia called me in quite a panic. Has anyone heard from her? I've dialed and texted and the old girl is not returning anything."

The others shook their heads.

Kiyoko considered. "She must have worked it out, then. Or so I hope."

"Maybe we can check in on her in a little bit?" Alexa suggested. "Meanwhile, where have you been and where did you get those clothes? It's such a different look for you. Not bad, but . . ."

"The shoes are bad," Gen said.

Kiyoko ran her hands through her hair. "I had to babysit for Ice Daddy's wife and her little babies threw up all over me."

"There's a lot of that going around," Alexa said.

"Well, it is at the W, that's for certain. So she and her friends dressed me. And then I saw Cody."

"Oooh." Alexa clapped her hands. "How is he?"

"Fine," Kiyoko said. "Could hardly keep his hands off me, of course."

"Of course," Alexa said.

"We had a really good time, too," Charlotte said. "Trey, Gen, Naomi, and I coordinated the Beauty sections

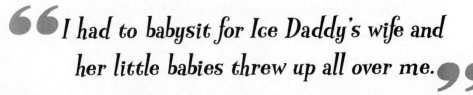

**66***I had to babysit for Ice Daddy's wife and her little babies threw up all over me.***99**

for the website and the double issue. We made up all these models to look like ice sculptures. It was amazing."

Alexa was so pleased to hear the confidence in Charlotte's tone. She also noticed Gen's slight frown of displeasure, as if she had lost her single adoring fan.

Gen nodded. "We saw Tatyana." Tatyana Milova was the group's model friend.

"That's so wonderful. I'll see you later. I have to go online at once," Kiyoko said, heading for the circular stairway.

Alexa knew something was up with her. She followed after her into their room. But Kiyoko sat down and pulled on her earphones, a sure indication that she was going to work on some music, so Alexa drifted over to Mel and Gen's room.

Mel was sitting at her desk, typing furiously on her laptop. Alexa wondered if it was the script or her homework. She was grateful that she had no interest in becoming a writer. It looked lonely and boring.

"Hi," Mel said, looking up at her. "I Googled the make of your camera so we could buy a replacement to give to Mother Michael. It's kind of hard to find." She caught her lower lip between her teeth. "And it's expensive."

She came around behind Mel as her friend clicked on a camera ad. Mel wasn't kidding. It was expensive. "It's at a store on Forty-Second Street," Alexa said.

"We could order it online and have it delivered or go pick it up," Mel told her. She raised a brow. "Then you could leave it on her office door stoop. Or have your friend Mary Beth sneak it where she'll see it."

"What if Chrissie returns it?" Alexa asked. "Then there will be two cameras."

"Maybe the store will take it back."

Alexa stared at the screen. "Maybe you could ask if they need an extra waitress at the restaurant. I'll need to make some money."

Just then, Kiyoko bounded through the doorway.

"Two huge things to tell you," she announced. "First of all, I just sent my music file to Cody to work on. We're going to burn a CD and give it to Donato soonest."

"That is so cool," Alexa said. "I'm so happy for you."

"Second, Miko just checked in. She and Lily will be here Saturday for the *Flirt* show."

"Wow!" Mel said. "You must be so excited!"

"*Ay!*" Alexa added. "You get to hang out with *Lily*?"

"Such is my life," Kiyoko said sweetly.

"I meant excited about your sister coming!" Mel said.

"That's brill, too, of course," Kiyoko said. She let her head fall back. "Gods, I'm tired."

"Kiyoko, I have a favor to ask of you," Alexa said,

suddenly very embarrassed.

She explained the whole camera incident. Kiyoko was completely, utterly, totally shocked.

"Why on the shining green planet would Top Penguin think that you stole your own camera?"

Alexa heaved another sigh. "She assumes the worst of me. She saw my school records from back home and now she thinks I'm the worst person alive. She said I'd have a clean slate, but really, there's no such thing."

"If Alexa can get a substitute camera to her, though, she can stay in school," Mel explained.

"And you need some purchasing power? I'm in, lads." Kiyoko gestured to the computer. "Put that bloody thing in your shopping cart."

"Oh, *thank* you," Alexa murmured. "You are saving my life."

"Done," Mel announced. "They'll deliver it by tomorrow afternoon."

"What if they don't?" Alexa fretted. "What if something happens?"

"Nothing will happen," Kiyoko said confidently.

## chapter ten

Thursday after school, Liv met Eli at the coffee house next to her building. He got her some iced chai and ordered an espresso for himself. He was wearing an NYU Film School T-shirt, some surfer shorts, and his horn-rimmed glasses, and he looked gorgeous.

Liv poured out her story to him and he nodded as if he were taking notes.

"They're so crazy," Liv said in conclusion. "But they also purchase loads of ad space from *Flirt*. So I can't exactly make a fuss. I'm caught in the middle."

"This is just like Hollywood," he said. "Especially the crazy part."

Unable to smile, she stirred her tea, listening to the sound of the ice against the spoon. "It's so ironic, Eli. It's wonderful that my earrings are in the show. In the fashion world, Fashion Week is the equivalent of the Oscar Awards ceremony. But *how* they got into the show is so . . . less than wonderful."

"Well, if it's enough that you knew they were yours, and they got in, I'd say just go with it. But I don't think it is enough. I think you don't want them to pass your work off as theirs."

She nodded.

## "Things will calm down eventually. I hope."

"So you either have to get them to give you credit, or refuse to let them use them."

"But then I'll have to tell Demetria that they're mine." She laid down her spoon. "And even if it doesn't cause a problem for *Flirt*, Demetria will go mental. She'll assume I went behind her back."

"Are you sure?" he asked her.

"Oh, yes." She drank her tea, but she was too nervous to taste it. Defeated, she set the cup down and said, "I have to go." She looked apologetic. "Ms. Bishop is having another party."

"All right. I know you'll figure this out," he said, as he pushed back at the same time she did. He gave her hand a squeeze. "It *is* pretty amazing that you got something into that show."

"Yes," she said. "It is."

"So Bishop's not wrong about you. And neither are James&Jane, even though they're creepy, lying flakes."

They walked out of the coffee house and into the sultry evening air. He kissed her and said, "Speaking of insane, I know this week is going to be crazy for you."

"Things will calm down eventually," she replied. Then she caught herself and smiled ruefully. "I hope."

It was six P.M., and Alexa and Mel took the elevator down to the lobby to check in with Sammy the doorman. No package from a camera store had arrived for Kiyoko Katsuda.

"Oh, no," Alexa said, paling. "It's not going to show up!" She began to panic.

"Alexa, stay calm," Mel said, even though she didn't feel very calm herself. "We'll check with the store."

They went back to the loft and phoned. The store was so sorry, but they were out of stock. Didn't their e-mail come through? No? So sorry.

*"Dios mio,"* Alexa said, sinking into Mel's chair.

"We'll find another store. Or a close match," Mel suggested. "We're in New York City, for heaven's sake. There are probably a thousand camera stores in the city."

Then Alexa's cell phone went off. *"Sí,"* she said, and Mel watched Alexa's expression morph into something fascinating. Deer-in-the-headlights meets unlimited-access-to-chocolate was the best she could come up with.

"Um, now?" Alexa said, her eyes growing huge. "Okay, Lynn. Of course."

She hung up. "Lynn wants me to work on a photo shoot tonight. It's Salma Hayek, Penélope Cruz, and

Luisana Lopilato together!" She whirled in a circle. "You cannot believe how famous Luisana Lopilato is in my country! Oh, my God, I'm so excited!"

Then she stopped whirling. "What about the camera?"

Mel said, "Don't worry, Alex. I'll handle it. I'll figure something out and get you a camera."

"*Ay,*" Alexa murmured. "*Gracias*, Mel. I'm too nervous. I'll have to borrow a *Flirt* camera again tonight." She glanced at the time displayed on her cell phone. "I have to go now!"

"It'll be all right," Mel said.

"That's what Kiyoko said," Alexa replied, sounding even more frantic.

ⓖ     ⓖ     ⓖ     ⓖ

On Lynn's orders (and with the promise of a reimbursement) Alexa cabbed it up to Bryant Park. She caught her breath as they came within sight of the cluster of tents. The two larger tents were like enormous white buildings; the two smaller ones sat in front of them. The park was swarming with people.

There was a white panel truck, the opened back revealing all kinds of photography lights, scrims, and gels. Two men and a woman, all in jeans, were removing the lights and carrying them to a location where another man stood with . . . could it be? Salma, Penélope, and Luisana. Alexa thought she might faint.

"Alexa, good," Lynn said. "Let me introduce you to Jon Liang. He's one of the most famous fashion photographers in the world."

*"Muchas gracias,"* Alexa said, her heart pounding as they approached the three *actrices latinas.* There they were, so beautiful and glamorous. Salma wore a copper strapless gown, Penélope was in scarlet, and Luisana was wearing gold. Demetria, Dwayne, and Liv were arranging the hem of Luisana's gown so that it made a full circle on the Oriental carpet spread beneath the actresses' feet, while makeup people were powdering their faces. Liv was actually speaking to Luisana!

"Alexa?" Lynn prodded.

Alexa stirred, realizing that she had spaced during her introduction to Jon Liang. She quickly recovered, pressing her hand across her chest and murmuring, "Mr. Liang, it's such an honor."

"No, no," he said proudly, because of course it was. He gestured to the scene around them. "What do you think?"

"It's so . . . busy," Alexa said, wondering how they would manage a photo shoot in all the chaos.

"That's what we're after," Jon Liang said, nodding to Lynn, who nodded back. "The chaos, the thrill of the hunt that is fashion!" He clapped his hands. "Let's get to work," he said, as he strode toward the actresses. "*Flirt's* not paying me thousands of dollars an hour to stand around."

Lynn followed after him, and Alexa followed after her. Speaking over her shoulder to Liv, Demetria walked over to a set of plastic bins. She picked up the topmost, read the label, and handed it to Liv. Then she took the second one and went back to the three beauties.

Jon Liang, Demetria, and Alexa approached just as Demetria reached into the bin and held up a pair of earrings. Liv's ruby and silver earrings!

"Oh, Liv!" Alexa cried with delight. "You're in the show, too!"

She beamed at her friend. But Liv grew pale and her neck muscles went taut, as if she had something caught in her throat.

Demetria frowned at the two of them. "What are you talking about?"

There was an awkward silence. Then Liv cleared her voice and said to Demetria, "May I speak to you in private for a moment?"

Demetria moved away from the truck. Liv caught up with her.

From the direction of the tents music blared, drowning out any possibility of overhearing the conversation. There was a moment where mentor and intern stood facing each other. Alexa assumed Liv was speaking. Then Demetria turned away from Liv, and Liv turned away from Demetria.

And then—¿como?—Liv just walked off, her shoulders hunched.

Alexa took a step in Liv's direction. Lynn murmured, "Stay here."

"But . . ." Alexa looked at Liv, who was now walking away so fast she was almost running.

Demetria came back toward Alexa. She glared at her, indicating they should take a little walk. When they were out of earshot, she asked to Alexa, "Did you know about the earrings all along?"

"About . . . ?" Alexa was terribly confused. "That Liv made them?"

Demetria narrowed her eyes. Before Alexa could say anything, Demetria waved her hand as if to erase the question. "We'll discuss it later," she said.

Alexa took one more look at Liv, but she was gone. As soon as she could, Alexa would call her and see what was going on. She knew it was about the earrings. She just didn't know why.

Alexa moved through the next couple of hours in a daze. She was worried about Liv, confused about the earrings . . . and very, very anxious about her camera.

⑨        ⑨        ⑨        ⑨

**FROM THE BLOG THAT ATE JAPAN!**
**OF KIYoKO!! GRRL WONDER!**

*saving flirt magazine one day at a time!!*
Written on: Thursday night—T-2 until the
Flirt fashion show!

1.  Kiyoko and Cody together again?

    We made some great cues online, and
now we are at Matsumoto Studios, 664
Fifth Avenue, to work on them in person.
I'm wearing my sari skirt and a baby T
silk-screened with *Vampire Team Sensei
Kristos*. It's one of their masterpieces. Cody
has on long pants with many pockets and a
plain white T-shirt and I just want to stare
at his muscles.

    He was over the moon that Donato
has offered to listen to some of our
work. Matsumoto & Kanno are like our
two uncles, allowing us to use their
sophisticated music programs while they
make tons of calls and entertain a constant
stream of guests. I am filled with green tea!

2.  K&C NOT together again?

    These guests: anime people I should
know! And Cody is already on a first-name
basis with many of them. Life in Tokyo has
moved on without me. One of my goals in

coming to New York in the first place was to meet Matsumoto and Kanno. *I was over the moon when I not only achieved that, but sold them some music.* But when I had a chance to fly back to Tokyo and work on a project with them, *I turned it down.* And Cody . . . here's this bright lad, awesome composer, and I let him fly off to Tokyo, and the reason I have time to write in this bloody blog on my laptop is he is having *another* phone conversation with that *mulher*, Mariko, supposedly about the fashion show. If he were an anime character, there would be big pulsating stars and hearts in the pupils of his eyes.

"Sorry," Cody said, grinning from ear to ear as he approached Kiyoko. *Treacherous male animal.*

She was sitting beside K&M's indoor koi pond, typing furiously away. She hit Save and made her personal reflections disappear.

"Oh, hello. Where were we?" Kiyoko asked sweetly.

"I think we should burn what we have," Cody suggested. "We've got some really good stuff. We can put a CD together. Unless you can directly e-mail our stuff to Donato?"

"Not at present," Kiyoko replied. She looked over at K&M, who were in big talks with some money guys. One of them had brought along a woman who desperately needed to eat, by the looks of her. She was swathed in high fashion. She was probably a model. Models made her think of Miko. She would be here soon!

"Kanno had a great suggestion," Cody continued. "He thought we should make a bunch of copies of the CD and pass them around when we have a chance. Donato is not the only world-famous singer here in New York."

"What a bloody good idea. Let's burn."

"How many do you think?" Cody asked her. "A dozen?"

Kiyoko snorted. "Thirty, at the least."

"Wow." Cody gazed at her with true respect. "You've been busy while I've been gone."

His phone trilled. She knew that tune. It was called "Mariko Wants You."

"I'll get it later," he said.

*Score one for Kiyoko*. She held up her hand. "Here's to the next step in our conquest of the music world!"

He high-fived her. Then, just as he was swooping toward her lips, Kanno held up the studio portable phone and said, "Cody, Mariko is calling."

*"Arigato gozaimashita,"* Cody said, giving a little apology grimace to Kiyoko as he want to get the phone.

A tiny apology, really. Barely noticeable.

Kiyoko growled deep in her throat. He didn't hear her. She didn't mean for him to.

As he darted away, she looked for Liv online. But Liv wasn't on. Mel, then.

**Mel_H: Hi! Excited! Just sent story to Jack. We agreed: I write it first, now he edits it. I think it's really good.**

**Kiyoko_K: I'm sure it's bloody brilliant. I'm at M&K w/ Cody. Phone! Belle! L8tr!**

**Mel_H: K!**

"Hey, got a peachy chore for you," Belle said into Kiyoko's ear. "Donato needs his outfit for the show sent over to The Closet. I can get a boring messenger to do it or I can send you."

"I kiss the ground you walk on," Kiyoko said.

Belle chuckled. "Call and let me know you got it. My voicemail will be on. I'm interviewing Sting in five."

She disconnected. Kiyoko sat for a moment of utter stillness, marveling at her mentor's fantastic sense of timing. Then she let out a whoop that got Cody's attention.

When he hung up on Mariko, she told him what Belle had given her to do.

"Can I come with you?" Cody asked like a big, hopeful puppy.

She said, "Of course," because that was what music partners did, even if Donato was a big flirt who might prefer to see her alone.

She wished she had time to slip into something more slippery, but she said, "Let's grab some blank CDs. We can burn them in the cab."

"Let's do one here before we go, just in case," he said, dashing over to a pile of jewel cases on the edge of a speaker. He picked up the lot and ran back to Kiyoko. She took one and inserted it in her built-in burner. *Zzzzip!* Done!

They ran over to M&K and explained what was happening. Both men bowed, wished them luck, didn't give a hoot about being paid for thirty measly blank CDs.

Kiyoko and Cody slid into the back of a cab and Cody put his arm around her shoulders. Could have been a boyfriend gesture, could have been pure nonsexual affection. Either way, she reflected on how she, Kiyoko Katsuda, had not been brought up to be so physical, and

**❝Cody put his arm around her shoulders. Could have been a boyfriend gesture, could have been pure nonsexual affection.❞**

yet she enjoyed it very much.

They got to Donato's building and made it past the doorman—same bloke—and into the elevator. As before, Donato himself opened the door to his lair of sensuality.

"*Bella mia,*" he said by way of greeting. Italian tonight, not Portuguese. She could live with that.

"We're here for your clothes," she said, grinning. "This is Cody Sammarkand, my music partner, and we brought you some music of ours." She boldly thrust the CD at him.

"Ah." He looked surprised but pleased as he took it from her. "Well, let's listen."

As he turned away, Kiyoko widened her eyes at Cody, whose mouth had dropped open. Then they nodded eagerly at each other and followed Donato to a laptop hooked up to two lovely external speakers.

He slid the disc in, and Cody grabbed Kiyoko's hand. He squeezed so tightly that it went a bit numb.

Their first cue issued from the speakers and danced around the room. *Oh my God!* Kiyoko thought. *It is so brill!*

Donato gestured for them to sit down. They perched as one on the edge of a black leather couch. His enormous weight of hair bobbed as he listened. Kiyoko could tell he was loving it.

All too soon, the CD ended. He actually looked disappointed!

"Nice. Very nice," he said. "Let me talk to some people, Kiyoko. And Cody." His hair bobbed again. "Try to set up some meetings for you."

It was her turn to wring the life out of Cody's hand. She said calmly, "That would be lovely, Donato. Let me give you our numbers and e-mails."

He whipped out his cell phone and said, "Go ahead."

She gave him her stuff. Then Cody gave him his stuff. Kiyoko couldn't quite make herself ask for his stuff. She wanted to make no request that he could refuse. She did not want "No" and "Kiyoko" to be wired together in his brain in any way. Cody must have understood; he didn't ask, either. He was letting her do most of the talking, probably because she had a prior relationship with Donato. After all, she had delivered his nougat.

They got his outfit—black silk pants, black short-sleeved silk top, black cowboy boots—she saw a trend! Then it was time to go.

He said, "I'll be in touch about your music," and then he ushered them out and shut the door.

In the hall, Kiyoko did a happy dance with Donato's clothes while Cody leaned his forehead against Donato's door and exhaled like a balloon.

"We have the most amazing lives," he murmured. Then he lifted his forehead and said, "Do you really think he'll do any of that?"

## *The universe, Kiyoko thought, is totally in love with me.*

"Of course! Our music is awesome!" Kiyoko cried. "Now, on the way to *Flirt*, let's burn some more CDs in case we run into anybody else."

"Do you think we will?" he asked her as they went back down in the elevator and cabbed it over to the *Flirt* offices.

With a stack of burned CDs in one hand and Donato's clothing in the other, they sailed down the busy-bee halls toward The Closet.

All alone and unaccompanied, Sting was walking toward them.

"Uh," Cody murmured, answering his own question.

*The universe,* Kiyoko thought, *is totally in love with me.*

## chapter eleven

It was after midnight when Alexa's cab pulled up to her building. After the shoot had wrapped, Demetria and Lynn had left with Jon Liang. Demetria had not spoken about Liv or her earrings again, and Alexa figured it was best not to bring it up. But as soon as she got back she was definitely going to talk to Liv if she could possibly rouse her.

Actually, she doubted Liv was asleep.

She went inside. Doorman George was on duty, and he gave her a wave as she made a dash for the elevator when the door opened.

Shane was inside. He looked as startled to see her as she was to see him, and he raised his brows as she entered.

"Hey," she said. "I just got back from a shoot. Salma Hayek, Penélope Cruz, and Luisana Lopilato."

"That's great." He smiled. "Was the tattooed lady there?"

"No, no," Alexa said. "She's in the show. This was a layout for our magazine."

"I see." He cocked his head. "I heard that Salma Hayek has bad skin. Scars or something."

*"What?"* She stared at him. "Where did you read such a horrible lie? She is perfect!"

"Huh. Then maybe it was Penélope Cruz." He shrugged. *"Someone* has bad skin."

"Well, it's no one I have seen," she assured him.

The elevator reached the fourth floor. He told her good night and left.

As the elevator reached the loft, her anxiety about Mother Michael and Liv caught back up with her. It had actually occurred to her to ask Lynn if they had any old digital cameras lying around unused, but she just couldn't bring herself to get anywhere near her problems with school.

The door slid open, and she stepped out.

She caught her breath.

Directly in front of her was one of the chairs from the kitchen table. And on it . . . a digital camera. And a note.

*Alexa,*

*Mel told me about your camera problem. This is the camera I tried to lend you earlier in the week. I have been wanting to get a new one, so it's yours for ten bucks.*

*—Nick*

Alexa was speechless.

And she was beyond grateful as she picked up the camera and cradled it against her chest. It was nearly identical to hers. And it would save her.

She started to go down the hall to thank Nick, but it was late. Then she thought about writing him a note, but she decided she would thank him in person the next time she saw him.

Now all that was left was Liv. But her friend was not online. Nor did she answer her cell phone.

*I hope she's asleep,* Alexa thought, *and not, like, on a plane to London or something.*

Everyone else was asleep, so Alexa quietly washed her face, brushed her teeth, and changed into her jammies. Then she made sure that her alarm was set, and fell asleep within seconds of climbing into bed.

In the morning, Alexa told Mel and Kiyoko about Liv. No one had heard from her, but they all agreed they would do their best to get in contact with her.

"Getting sent off a job by your mentor has got to hurt a tender lad like Olivia," Kiyoko said.

"I kind of wish Bishop would do that," Mel said. "Throw me off the job of writing the fashion show script. It's been two days since I submitted my final draft, and I still haven't heard from her." The confidence she had gained during her conversation with Nick was draining away with each passing hour.

"That is too bloody strange." Kiyoko slurped coffee laden with milk and sugar. "I suspect she is secretly an evil alien queen bent on destroying your mind."

"You read too much manga," Mel said affectionately.

"No such thing," Kiyoko retorted, grinning.

Alexa got to school well before the first bell. Nick's camera was in her backpack, and she considered taking it out before she knocked on Mother Michael's office door. But she was so nervous, she was afraid she might drop it.

"Come in," Mother Michael said, and Alexa pushed open the door.

The nun was sitting behind her desk. And Alexa's camera was sitting on top of it.

Alexa closed her eyes for a beat as the weight of the world rose off her shoulders. She croaked, "Do you know who took it?"

"Please see if it's damaged," Mother Michael said.

Alexa picked it up and turned it over, clicked buttons . . . and remembered that the memory card was missing. So she couldn't really put it through its paces.

She said, "It looks okay," which was not a lie. Reluctantly, she handed it back to Mother Michael.

"Keep it." Mother Michael paused. "Yes, I do know. The thief has been apprehended."

She pointed to a place behind Alexa, and Alexa turned to look. *Ay, caramba*. A security camera stared down at her from the left corner of the room.

"After your camera was taken, the police suggested I install that. It seems the thief had an attack of conscience and attempted to return your camera.

We caught the whole thing on tape," Mother Michael informed her. "She will not be back."

"W-who?" Alexa asked again. Her defenses sprang up, bracing herself for the other shoe to drop. What if Chrissie had told her about the missing memory card, perhaps in an attempt to avoid expulsion?

A wave of pain clouded the mother's features. "I would prefer not to disclose that information," Mother Michael said. After a beat, she added, "It's nearly time for your chemistry class."

"Yes, Mother."

As Alexa began to leave, the principal said, "And Alexa? I am sorry I doubted your word." She even looked sorry.

"No, Mother, I'm sorry that you couldn't trust me," Alexa said. And she meant it. No more pranking!

She hurried out of the room, down the hall, and into class. As she expected, Mary Beth was there.

And so was Chrissie.

*¿Que? It wasn't Chrissie who took it?*

She held up her camera so both girls could see it. Mary Beth nodded, her face cracking into a big grin. Chrissie gave her a long-distance high five.

Alexa slid into her chair in front of Mary Beth. Seconds later, Sister Andrew walked through the door from her office into the classroom and picked up her stick beside the periodic table.

> ## I guess she really, really, really didn't want you to have any pictures of her.

Mary Beth kicked Alexa's chair. "Told you it wasn't Chrissie," she whispered.

Alexa turned her head. "Do you know who it was?" she whispered.

"Who can explain what a covalent bond is?" Sister Andrew asked the class.

"Sister Pauline," Mary Beth mouthed.

Alexa's jaw dropped.

"I guess she really, really, really didn't want you to have any pictures of her," Mary Beth said.

"Why not?" Alexa whispered.

Mary Beth shrugged.

"Christine, do you know what a covalent bond is?" Sister Andrew said.

"How do you know it was Sister Pauline?" Alexa whispered.

"That's right! Very good, Christine."

*Whap!* against the chart!

᭢          ᭢          ᭢          ᭢

**From:** bishop@flirt.com
**To:** mel_h@flirt.com
**Subject:** Script

You did it. Good job.

—JB

     Mel floated to her locker. Floated. She had done it! She'd popped into the computer lab in between classes, and her heart had stopped when she saw Bishop's name in her inbox. After she'd read the e-mail, she'd whooped and opened the attachment. It was her script; Bishop had made a few tiny changes and e-mailed it to everyone connected to the show—with *by Melanie Henderson* prominently displayed on page one! She didn't know how it had happened. She'd taken a step away, gotten what she needed, then come back into what was happening around her.

     She couldn't wait to tell . . . Jack?

     Or Nick?

     *The world?*

     "Hey." It was Jack, trotting up to her as she closed her locker and began to walk to their workshop class. She hadn't seen him since Wednesday—all communication about their short story had happened through e-mail, Jack assuring her that he was working on his edit of her first draft, which was "excellent." Excellent felt like the truth. She had loved the story she'd sent him.

*I've got my writing groove back!*

"Hi," she said.

"I've almost got the draft done." He patted his backpack. "It's really shaping up. We can talk about it in class."

"Shaping up?" She made a face. "That sounds kind of dire."

"It was a little rough," he replied. At her startled look, he laughed and said, "I just smoothed the edges a little." He mimicked typing.

"Oh." She couldn't help a little surge of anxiety. "Well, can I take a look now?"

"Sure." He reached into his backpack and pulled out a thick pile of pages. "Like I said, I'm almost done."

"Okay." She took the pages. She was about to look through them when the bell rang. It was time for their workshop class.

Ms. Kaneshige smiled at her and Jack as they entered the class. She said, "How's the collaboration working out?"

"Like a dream," Jack said.

ⓖ　　ⓖ　　ⓖ　　ⓖ

*Like a nightmare.*

As Ms. Kaneshige lectured on characterization, Mel read the pages. Her story, her beautiful story, was gone. Jack had taken out nearly every word she'd written and substituted his own. There was nothing of her in it.

Her stomach was a tight ball. Her hands trembled.

Then it was workshopping time, and the Poes moved to their circle of desks. Ms. Kaneshige said, "I'd like Mel and Jack to go first today, to talk about how their partnership is going."

"We're not quite done," Jack said. "See, she wrote the first draft and now I'm editing it. But I haven't gotten to the end yet."

Mel took a breath. She looked at Jack and said, "How can you not be done? You've rewritten all of it."

He chuckled as if he didn't believe her. He gestured to the manuscript. "Only here and there."

"No." She sifted through the pages, scanning all his edits, looking for more than a phrase here or there that she had written. "There's hardly anything I wrote left."

"You were the catalyst," Jack said. "I took what you wrote and tweaked it."

"To make it sound like *your* stuff."

"No. To make it better." He smiled at her. "Which I did."

Mel looked through the pages again. "This is all

you. There's no . . . me."

"There's no *Flirt*," he corrected. "Maybe it was working on the script for that show that messed you up, but this story was . . . crappy."

*Omigosh. How can he say that?* She was completely mortified.

"Okay, time out here," Ms. Kaneshige said.

Mel started to disengage.

*Maybe he's right. Maybe it is crappy.*

And then she remembered what Nick had said about Bishop and storms. All those risk-takers, those people daring to live their big dreams. *They* would stand up for their work.

She handed the pages back to him and said to Ms. Kaneshige, "My story was not crappy. It just wasn't what Jack wanted to write."

"You just don't know how to work with someone else," Jack said, holding the pages in both his hands. "Someone with a strong personality like mine."

Mel stared at him. A strong personality? He had nothing on Bishop.

She said, "You don't know me at all, Jack." She looked back at their teacher. "I don't want to discuss this in front of the group," she said firmly.

"All right," Ms. Kaneshige said, waving her hands. "Obviously, this was an experiment that failed." She grimaced. "I'll have to ask each of you to turn in your version of your story, good?"

Mel silently nodded. Her stomach was in knots. It had taken everything in her to speak up, and now that she had done it, she was pretty shaken.

After class, Jack tried to catch up to her as she walked quickly out of the room.

"Hey, I guess I overdid it," he said, tapping her on the shoulder.

She licked her lips. "Yes. You did."

She moved on.

ⓖ     ⓖ     ⓖ     ⓖ

"We snuck in and watched the camera tape, that's how," Mary Beth told Alexa after school. They were walking down the main corridor, three across. "And we saw her, same as Mother Michael saw her when *she* watched the camera tape."

Chrissie nodded. "There was some other stuff on there, too." She snickered and Mary Beth snorted. It was the sort of glee a fellow prankster could appreciate.

"What kind of stuff?" Alexa asked.

"Want to watch it, too?" Mary Beth asked.

*No more pranking,* Alexa reminded herself, just

**❝ It was the sort of glee a fellow prankster could appreciate. ❞**

before she said, "Of course I do!"

However, there was no chance that day. As soon as she changed out of her uniform, it was back to work for Lynn.

☺      ☺      ☺      ☺

"Kiyoko," Belle, well, bellowed, in Kiyoko's ear, "where the hell are you?"

Seated beside Cody on Donato's black leather couch, Kiyoko jumped up and took her cell phone into the hall.

"Oh," she said. "Hi, Belle."

"You need to be down here. I'm at the tent. We have to be out of here in an hour."

"So sorry," Kiyoko said. The thing was, Donato had invited them over to "have a meeting about your music." There were about a dozen other people in his penthouse; Kiyoko wasn't certain who they were, except that they were "from my label." That sounded promising. But so far, all that had happened was that everyone had a couple of drinks (Kiyoko stuck to diet tonic water) and chitchatted. She kept delaying her exit, wondering if they would finally get to the point.

"On my way, chief," she said.

They disconnected. She walked to the end of the hall and motioned Cody toward her. He came over and she said, "I have to go."

"We haven't gotten anywhere," he said, frustrated.

"*You* don't have to go," she replied, crossing her eyes. "Work it, Cody. At least get them to listen to it."

He nodded. "Okay."

They walked back into the room. "I need to go to Belle," she said, "but Cody can stay and discuss things."

"Oh, what a shame," Donato said. "But we'll see you soon, *sì*?"

"*Sì,*" she said firmly.

Kiyoko was out the door and down to the tents. It was the day before the *Flirt* fashion show and the place was crazy, flooded with media personalities doing on-camera preshow bits. She headed for the *Flirt* tent with her big satchel slung over her shoulder. It was loaded with freshly burned CDs. She and Cody had already gone through the first thirty. Every time she saw *anyone* connected with the music industry, she gave them one.

She flashed her *Flirt* badge at the security guard and dashed inside the enormous tent. It reminded her of the circus. Scaffolds had been erected to position the stationary banks of speakers. Up on the runway, Kiyoko saw her boss and the sound crew with the *Flirt* show's own equipment.

The crew was a mixture of the guys provided by the group that organized Fashion Week, and a whole slew of individual guys provided by the various celebs who were going to sing in the show. They kind of hated one another, mostly, everyone jostling to get the best deal for their individual star, and Kiyoko thought the entire plan was nutty. No wonder Belle was so cranky.

However, not as cranky as the Flirtistas, once they'd heard from Liv what had happened between her, James&Jane, and Demetria. Demetria had told Liv that James&Jane got to pass the earrings off as their own, if that was what it took to keep them buying ad space from *Flirt*, and Liv was to chalk it up to a lesson learned the hard way.

"Kiyoko!" Belle shouted. *Shouted?*

"Here," Kiyoko said, dashing toward her.

"Either show up on time, or don't show," Belle said.

*Yikes!*

@ @ @ @

Saturday morning! The day of the *Flirt* fashion show!

Jo Bishop wanted to ensure that everyone walking away from New York's Fashion Week would have one final impression on their minds—in one word, *Flirt*. So the crafty CEO had timed the show to end at the stroke of midnight—the exact end of Fashion Week. But there was still plenty to be done before then.

As a reward for their hard work all week, Bishop had invited the interns to a *Flirt*-sponsored VIP brunch. Mel and the five other interns stood around Bishop, who was holding court in a roped-off area. Champagne was flowing. Music was pounding. Media stars—movies, TV, music—paraded in haute couture. A thousand cameras click-click-clicked.

Mel was intrigued. She'd been behind-the-scenes all week, and this was far more thrilling than she ever could have anticipated. Fashion Week was about risks, daring . . . and huge amounts of money. Everything about it was expensive: the tents themselves, the clothes, the models. Kiyoko's sister was going to make more walking the runway in their fashion show that evening than Mel's parents combined made in two months. And supermodel Lily's salary could probably pay for a small island.

She looked at the smiles and felt a rush of intense admiration for everyone involved in this crazy, wild industry: They all had gone through an awful lot of storms. So far they were the survivors. But they might not be, next season. Some would fail, and new designers and houses would struggle to take their place.

She murmured, "Wow."

And somehow, through all the noise, Bishop heard her. She turned to Mel and gave her a long hard look. Mel flushed beneath her scrutiny, but then Bishop smiled as if she knew exactly what Mel was thinking and said, "Now you know why I was so hard on you about the script."

Mel almost laughed aloud. She said, "Why haven't you given up on me?"

"*Melanie,*" was all Bishop said in reply.

Then the moment was over. But Mel was thrilled. It was as if she had learned the secret to being a writer.

◉     ◉     ◉     ◉

Three hours later, back at the loft, Liv, Mel, and Kiyoko waited for Miko and Lily to arrive. Alexa was on another photo shoot and would join them a little later.

The three friends were decompressing after the excitement of the morning. Kiyoko had ordered scads of pizzas—both she and Miko had a fetish—and Emma had made her renowned cheesecake before she'd left for a party of her own—old friends from her fashion photography days.

Liv was not in a party mood. Demetria had told her not to "burden" Ms. Bishop with the "situation" about her earrings, and she had obeyed. As far as Liv knew, her "mentor" had not "burdened" James&Jane with any discussion of them, either. Demetria also assumed Liv had snuck them into the accessory bins for the photo shoot at Bryant Park. How else to explain their mysterious appearance?

"Miko!" Kiyoko shouted, staring down at her

BlackBerry. "Battle stations, everyone! They're approaching the garage!"

Due to Lily's extreme fame, the two models were being snuck into the building. Their limo would be driven into the parking garage, and Kiyoko would take the elevator down to them. Then the two models plus a security guard would take the elevator straight up.

Kiyoko hopped into the elevator and went down to greet her sister.

Mel turned to Liv and said, "I just read an interview Miko did for *Lucire*. She sounds like Kiyoko on steroids."

Despite her gloomy mood, Liv chuckled. "You do have a way with words, Mel."

"It's nice to see you smiling," Mel returned. "I know you've got a lot on your mind, but if you could just imagine it surrounded by a pink bubble that drifts up toward the moon . . ."

"Ommm," Liv teased, closing her eyes, tilting back her head, and pressing her thumbs and middle fingers together.

The elevator arrived and the door opened.

Enter the Katsuda dragons.

First the bodyguard exited, and then Kiyoko leaped out of the elevator, shrieking, *"Aiya!"*

Assuming a karate battle stance, Kiyoko was wearing a new black silk baseball jacket—clearly a present from big sis. Somewhere between leaving the flat

## "Miko had affected a heavy cyborg-geisha look."

and returning, she had wound her hair into a messy bun stabbed in place with two chopsticks and a crazy-colorful red and yellow bandana with *Make Me Your Apprentice!* emblazoned over a kaleidoscope of anime characters.

"All clear," she informed the bodyguard. Then she turned to the girls, spread open her left arm toward the elevator, and said, "Ta da!"

Then . . . *la* Miko burst out like a hurricane. Taller than Kiyoko, with longer black hair than Kiyoko, in more makeup than Kiyoko—Miko had affected a heavy cyborg-geisha look, with a pale face, black brows, a bit of bronze shading around her eyes, and dark bronze lip stain dotting the middle one-third of her mouth.

She was dressed from the crown of her head to the tips of her toes in bronze and metallic acid green—green and bronze rosettes sprinkled in her waist-length hair; an enormous collar of bronze around her neck, very Masai warrior; a spaghetti-strap top of bronze; and a miniskirt that covered perhaps one-eighth of her tremendously long legs. Her bronze leather lace-up sandals were four-inchers minimum, and her toenails were decorated with tiny dots of bronze.

"Here she is!" Kiyoko sang out. "Fresh from the

set of *Troy*!"

Miko guffawed, throwing back her head. She strode into the loft and said, "Kiki, darling, what am I doing in Paris? I should move in with you."

"Not at the prices these blokes charge," Kiyoko shot back, and the two sisters fell to laughing like big strappin' drunk cowboys. The interns did not pay rent, and Liv figured that must have been the source of the merriment.

Then Kiyoko grabbed Miko's hand and held it out as if Miko were a marionette, and said, "Meet my mates. Mel, our hippie writer, and Liv, the aristo designer."

"How d'you do," Miko said in a very clipped British accent as she shook first with Mel, and then with Liv. "Seen you around at the shows and things with your parents," she said to Liv. Her grip nearly crushed Liv's fingers.

"Indeed. It's nice to actually meet you," Liv said politely.

*"Nice,"* Kiyoko mimicked, wagging her finger at Liv. "Winnie-the-Pooh."

"Pay no attention to my sister. She's a rude Brazilian," Miko said.

Kiyoko stuck out her tongue.

Kiyoko's joy at reuniting with her sister was palpable, and Liv was wistful. She had no siblings, and she and her parents were not close.

"We have pizza and cheesecake," Kiyoko told Miko, then turned to Mel and Liv and said, "Get this: Lily is a no-show."

Liv's lips parted in shock. Mel's eyes widened. Liv said. "What?"

Miko said, "Is there meat on the pizza?"

*"Hai-hai,"* Kiyoko said in Japanese, and rattled off some more sentences. She added, "Pardon our rudeness. Unlike me, my sister actually spent a good part of her childhood in Japan. As she is jet-lagged, she's more comfortable with that lingo."

Miko rolled her eyes. "Please. My English is impeccable."

"Oh, by the shining green planet." Kiyoko made as if to swoon. "She knows the best big words in several highly commercial languages. I want to be you, Miko-*chan*!"

"I know," Miko said serenely, as she made a beeline for the table loaded with pizza and Emma's cheesecake.

Examining the spread, she said, "Let's eat the cheesecake first. Yes, Lily is not coming. I have a personal, handwritten note of apology for Gianna." She picked up a knife and said, "How many people want cheesecake? I can cut it into fifths." She smiled at her bodyguard, who had taken up residence beside the elevator. He did not smile back. He reminded Liv of the silent guards at the Tower of London.

## 66More people are coming, you right piglet.99

"More people are coming, you right piglet," Kiyoko told her sister.

Liv blanched. "How can she simply not come?"

Miko grabbed a bright orange plate, cut a hunk of cheesecake, and laid it lovingly onto the plate.

"Here, Mel," Miko said, then turned to Liv. "She is exhausted. She simply cannot go on. She's giving up modeling." She pressed her fingers across her prominent collarbones and sighed theatrically. "And I think there's a French painter involved."

"Ha! Painters," Kiyoko said, giving Mel an eye.

"Well, she'll be sued," Mel said, her cheeks turning a lovely shade of pink.

"Six ways to Sunday, is that how they say it?" Miko asked. "But . . . she's Lily."

"Is she really giving up modeling?" Mel persisted.

"One does not know the ways of Lily," Miko said with a shrug.

"Wait until you see Charlanne Papel's tattoo," Kiyoko said. "They're still going to need someone to wear Lily's dress."

"Gen will offer," Liv said.

"I doubt it," Mel put in, as Miko handed her a plate. "I think she's tired of being told that she's too short."

The bodyguard touched his ear and said, "Okay, hold on." He looked at the girls and said, "Alexa wants to come up."

"She inhabits this domain," Kiyoko told him. "She may rise."

"Yes, go ahead," the guard told his ear.

Miko continued cutting up and serving the cheesecake. Liv accepted hers, along with a fork. It was sheer heaven. Emma had been thinking of selling her cheesecakes as a business, and Liv highly approved.

Miko handed a piece to her bodyguard and said, "Here, Lazlo, darling. Devour." She smiled at the others. "Lazlo scared away a horrid reporter. The man had the cheek to say he lived here."

Liv said, "What reporter?"

Miko rolled her eyes. "Oh, he's awful. A scandal-monger. He stirs things up, tries to get the dirt on people, you know? Writes for all the worst papers in England."

The elevator arrived and the door opened. Alexa came into the loft as Miko said, "You'd have heard of him, Liv. His name's Sean Mirrus."

"Alexa, hi," Mel greeted her.

"Oh dear, he's dreadful," Liv said, giving Alexa a little wave. "Of course I've heard of him! He's plagued my family for years."

"*Dios mio*," Alexa said, looking ill. "Shane Morris?"

"No. But close. Sean Mirrus," Liv said. "Miko, this is Alexa Veron, from Buenos Aires."

Alexa swallowed. "Tall, big dark brown eyes? Tan?"

"Known for his tan," Miko said, turning to see Alexa for the first time. "Oh my God! You're beautiful!" Miko cried, staring at Alexa. "*You* can wear the dress!"

"*Ay*, no," Alexa moaned, sinking down onto the floor and burying her face in her hands.

"What's wrong?" Liv asked Alexa.

"Shane Morris," Alexa said.

"Oh, poo, he's nothing." Miko waved a hand as if to squash a mosquito dead. "Let's talk about Alexa's modeling career. Have you signed with an agency? I need to show you to my manager."

Alexa blinked at her. "Are you Kiyoko's sister?"

"*Hai-hai,*" Miko said cheerfully. "Now, first we need to cut your hair."

"*Por favor,*" Alexa said, stricken. "Please, we need to discuss Shane Morris."

ⓖ    ⓖ    ⓖ    ⓖ

The pizzas and cheesecake were forgotten as Alexa tried to remember every single thing she had told "Shane Morris" each time she had run into him. They had decided that he knew exactly who she and the others were, and he was digging for dirt.

"And then I said a model had gotten a big tattoo and we had to 'lose' her dress. And that she looked like a monster."

"Yikers," Miko said.

Alexa shook her head. "I *knew* I shouldn't say anything. I had a funny feeling all along."

> **You're not the first to be fooled by him.**

"He can be very charming," Miko consoled her. "You're not the first to be fooled by him. That's why he's so good at what he does."

"Moving to damage control," Kiyoko cut in. "What are we going to do?" She hopped to her feet. "I've got it."

She walked out of the sunken living room to the elevator and pressed the button.

"What are you doing?" Miko said.

"I'm going to parlay with that rotter."

⊙     ⊙     ⊙     ⊙

Kiyoko zoomed down to the car park, nosed around, went out into the street, and rounded the corner. Shane Morris was not loitering anywhere.

She went to the lobby, to find Sammy at his console.

She said, "Did that guy from 4A happen to sneak in here?"

Sammy said, "Yeah. He came in a couple of minutes ago and took the stairs because I explained the elevator was temporarily unavailable. Because of Miko, but of course I didn't say that to him." He raised his brows. "Is there a problem?"

"Stay tuned," Kiyoko said as she flew back into the lift and got out on the fourth floor. She ran to apartment A and pounded on the door.

There *had* to be a governing deity . . . because Sean Mirrus opened the door himself!

Kiyoko said, "We're onto you, us on the top floor."

He frowned. "I have no idea what you're talking about."

"Stow it," she said. "You cannot use anything my loftmate said to you because it was all off the record."

"I still don't understand."

*Oooh, the lying creep.*

"I will give you money."

Then he smiled. "You don't have enough."

"You don't know who I am."

"Yes, I do, Ms. Katsuda."

*Oh.*

She took a breath. "Then you know that I am a member of a very wealthy and influential family. And that I intern in the Entertainment department. And that I am very charming and make friends. So here it is: I will get you an exclusive interview with Donato, in return for your word that you won't use anything my loftmate gave you."

He snorted. "You can't give me that." He narrowed his eyes. "But you *can* give me Lily."

"He and I are working together," she informed him, ignoring the Lily portion of the conversation. She was miffed that he had not demanded to speak to Miko. Not that Miko would. "That's much better than what you have."

"Please. Charlanne Papel is *huge*."

Aha! She almost screamed, she was so happy. She knew at that moment that Alexa was saved. "That tat's yesterday's news," Kiyoko said. "Everyone's been gossiping about it. But *Donato* . . ."

"You can't pull that off," he said uncertainly. "Give me Lily."

"Lily's not available," she said, as she whipped out her cell. "I'll have him on this phone in one hour. I'll come back and you can talk to him."

He looked intrigued. "One hour. And then I'm filing my story."

"Good." She thought about shaking his hand, but he was completely disgusting.

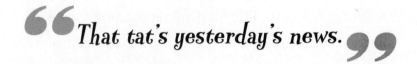

**" *That tat's yesterday's news.* "**

Kiyoko decided she should perform her next task in private, so she went back down to the lobby, past Sammy, and outside. She dialed her directory service and got herself connected to the *Post*'s hot-tip desk. Belle had taught her how to leak stories with the best of them.

So she told the story of Charlanne Papel and her tattoo, and the dress, and all of it. She was actually an intriguing combination of frightened and excited as she spilled her guts.

When she was finished, she went back inside and said to Sammy, "That lad from 4A? Scummy reporter looking for dirt to print. A word to the wise."

Sammy cocked his head. "Interesting. The renter on the lease for 4A is a journalism prof at CUNY."

"Well, the prof's harboring a force of evil," Kiyoko replied.

"Be assured, Katsuda-san, I am always discreet about the sixth floor."

"We are grateful," she said, bowing.

Kiyoko zoomed back up to the loft and reported in to the troops.

"You called the *Post*?" Mel asked, utterly shocked. "Keeks, are you crazy?"

"As a loon," Kiyoko said. Then she frowned. "I don't think I meant to say that."

"But the fallout," Liv said, making a face. "Charlanne Papel will be furious. She'll demand to know how it was leaked."

"Someone else was talking to Mirrus," Kiyoko said. "Maybe someone at *Flirt*. Because he knew it was Charlanne Papel, and *you* didn't tell him that. Correct?"

"Yes, *muy* correct. I never said her name," Alexa insisted. "I was very careful."

"You see?" Kiyoko said. "Now, if he names you as a source, Alexa, deny, deny, deny."

"I will," she said.

"Very impressive," Miko drawled. "*Omedeto gozaimasu*, Kiko-chan." Then she said to Alexa, "I am serious, luv. You are exquisite. You should be a model. You should wear the dress Lily was going to wear."

"Thank you," Alexa said, dipping her head.

"You don't believe me. You don't think it could happen," Miko accused her gently. "Well, watch this. I'm taking you with me when I deliver Lily's message to Gianna." She looked at her sister. "You come, too, so she won't be nervous."

Alexa looked a little dizzy. She said to Miko, "You *are* serious."

"I am," Miko informed her.

As they walked toward the dining area, Miko said to Liv, "You're the one with the jewelry, yes? Tatyana told me about you."

"Yes," Liv said quietly. "That's me."

"Listen to this," Kiyoko said to her sister. She told her the entire story of James&Jane.

"That's awful," Miko said, when Kiyoko was finished. "Oh, that's just bloody wrong."

"And yet," Mel said. Alexa nodded.

"Well . . ." Miko thought a moment. "If I'm told to wear those ruby earrings, I'll flat-out refuse. *I'll* walk off the show."

"That's very admirable, big sister, but all that will happen is that they will sue *you* and replace *you*," Kiyoko said as she grabbed up a floppy, oily piece of meat-laden pizza.

Miko huffed. "Well, how about this, then? As models, we'll be interviewed by the media, and we'll be going to lots of parties." She smiled at Kiyoko, who looked thrilled at the thought of lots of parties.

"I'll get all my friends to wear Liv's jewelry and chat her up," Miko went on, turning to Liv. "We won't cross the line Demetria's set for you, but we'll get you some publicity, at the very least. And I know a designer, very new, very . . . aggressive." She giggled. "He's an aristo, French, has tons of connections. Plus, we're snogging."

"Thank you," Liv murmured, moved nearly to tears. "So very much."

"We Katsudas are champions of the downtrodden," Kiyoko informed her.

> **"** *And I know a designer, very new, very . . . aggressive. He's an aristo, French, has tons of connections. Plus, we're snogging.* **"**

"Power to the people," Mel said, raising her vegetarian pizza slice in salute.

*"Banzai!"* Kiyoko cried, doing the same with her meaty slice. "To Alexa and Liv!"

*"Banzai!"* Mel cried.

Everyone raised their pieces of pizza. Including Liv.

## chapter twelve

On the way to the *Flirt* offices, Alexa was too nervous and excited to think. Kiyoko was humming beneath her breath as she, Miko, and Alexa were ushered to where Gianna Russo waited, and Alexa's heart beat in time to the complicated rhythm.

The dark-haired, sad-eyed designer greeted them in a black sheath and black sandals. She kissed Miko on the cheeks and said to Kiyoko, "How lovely to see you again, my dear."

Gianna's expression remained unreadable as Miko filled her in on the Lily no-show. Then she fastened her eyes on Alexa. Her brows shot up and she cocked her head, nodding.

*"Bella, bella, bella."* She said to Miko, "I will never forgive Lily. I will never use her again."

"Ah, that is sad," Miko said sincerely.

Gianna smiled at Alexa. "Not so sad."

ⓖ    ⓖ    ⓖ    ⓖ

Kiyoko headed to her cube, checked her voicemail and her e-mail. There was no word from Donato.

She texted Cody.

**KIYoKO!!!: Doko ni?**
**DJCody: Matsu Studios. working on**
   **project. You?**
**KIYoKO!!!: At the office.**
**DJCody: Do something for dinner?**

She was about to tell him how brill that would be when Belle said, "Kiyoko? What are you doing? I need you."

Kiyoko took a breath. "How long will you need me?"

Belle swiveled around from her desk. "Depends on how long these podcasts take."

**KIYoKO!!!: Not sure when I will**
   **get free. I'll contact you later.**
   **daijoubu?**

"Kiyoko?" Belle asked sharply. "Are you here or not?"

"Yes, ma'am, I am here," Kiyoko said, stowing her BlackBerry. She moved quickly to Belle's side. "Your wish is my command."

　　　　🌀　　🌀　　🌀　　🌀

While Belle and Kioyoko worked, Belle got a call

from a celebrity who was in dire need of a little bit of VIP treatment. Kiyoko knew Belle had an interview scheduled with another A-lister for later on. She listened, fascinated, as the editor deftly invited Miss B-list along for the A-list plan. It was brilliant: the B-lister would be thrilled, the A-lister would be flattered. Genius, sheer genius.

Then Belle said, "You should come, too, Kiyoko. Eight o'clock, the SoHo Grand, you got it?"

"Yes," Kiyoko said, as her cell phone vibrated in her pocket.

She excused herself to go to the women's room and checked the message.

### DJCody: DONATO!!!!!!! Chateau Chat 6:30!!

"Oh. My. Nondenominational. God," Kiyoko breathed. Finally. It was almost six now. She typed him back that that was fine and went back to Belle. She took a breath, smiled like a burdened schoolgirl, and said, "I do have a little homework tonight. If I might go do that, and meet you there?"

"Oh." Belle glanced away from her computer and looked at Kiyoko. "It's Saturday. And I thought your school didn't assign homework?"

"They changed their minds," Kiyoko said.

Belle smiled wryly. "Got it. Sure. Go get it done."

Kiyoko turbo-charged back to the loft to change into a better outfit. Chateau Chat was, after all, one of the hottest new restaurants in all of NYC. Kiyoko had not yet been, but she was pleased as punch to be going.

She cabbed it downtown. She was singing under her breath when the taxi pulled to the curb. Then she nearly choked on her own melodious syllables.

*Mariko* was with Cody. She was all dolled up in a little shift, strappy sandals, and a messy bun. She looked fantastic.

For a moment, Kiyoko thought about telling the cab to drive on. But she kept her head, saying "Here," thrusting money at the driver; as calmly as she could, she stepped out of the cab.

Cody flushed beet-red and gave her a little wave. He said, "I hope you don't mind. Yuko had a thing and Mariko was alone."

"Can't have that," Kiyoko said, as Mariko lifted her chin and smiled sourly at her. Her heart was pounding. and if she were an anime character, little daggers and surface-to-Mariko missiles would be shooting out of her pupils.

They were ushered into a private room. Donato

> 66 *Then she nearly choked on her own melodious syllables.* 99

was there with a bunch of people. Kiyoko recognized three of them from their previous meet-and-greet at his place.

"*Bella* Kiyoko," he said, air-kissing her. "I think tonight the talent man is coming." He smiled and gestured to some plates of starters on the table. "Have some escargot."

Kiyoko plopped down in the only empty seat next to Donato. Cody and his *date* could fend for themselves.

More people came. None of them was the talent man. Skinny models arrived, disdaining anything that looked like food. Some famous singers arrived. Everyone kept noshing on starters. Donato ordered lots of champagne and people started to get a little silly.

Kiyoko checked her watch. *Yikes*. It was nearly seven thirty.

She said, "Um, this talent man?"

"Soon," Donato promised. He poured her a glass of champagne.

She looked over at Cody and Mariko, who were yakking nose-to-nose like they were planning their wedding reception.

*I had the gig,* she thought. She was filled with regret. *If I had gone to Tokyo . . . but if this thing works out with Donato . . . this thing that never seems to work out with Donato . . . if I'm extra-nice to Cody . . .*

*. . . I had the gig. I had it.*

> ## "Belle needs me and she is my supreme commander."

And then a little voice inside her said, *You still have a gig. At* Flirt. *So go to it.*

*But this is a bigger gig. This one is the one that will change my life.*

*Keeks, you have those all the time!*

She jumped to her feet. She said to Donato, "I am sorry, but I have to go. Belle needs me and she is my supreme commander."

"Hail, Caesar," Donato said, chuckling. He whipped out his cell phone. "I'll tell her to let you stay."

"No!" Kiyoko pleaded. Heads turned in her direction. "No," she said more calmly. "I promised, and I need to go."

Donato shrugged. "You'll miss the talent man."

"Cody can handle it, yes?" she asked, gazing at her music partner. Her music partner and nothing more. Because she had not been there, and Mariko had.

It hurt. Badly.

"Okay," Cody said. "I'll call you."

"That would be . . . brill," Kiyoko choked out.

Then she left.

ⓖ　　ⓖ　　ⓖ　　ⓖ

When Kiyoko got to the *Flirt* hospitality suite at the hotel, Belle was waiting at the entrance. She cocked her head and said, "Homework, huh?"

"No," Kiyoko replied, slumping. "Schmoozing on your time. How did you know?"

"Donato called and said to tell you that 'the talent man' had just canceled. Speaking of talent men, I've been meaning to talk to you about all the CDs you've been passing out."

"Not cool?" Kiyoko asked, making a face.

"Not very. There's targeting your market and there's flinging doubloons at Mardis Gras."

Kiyoko had no idea what she was saying exactly, but she got the gist. She was a little over the top with all the pass-outs. She said, "I'll do better."

Belle grinned at her and opened the door. "Don't sweat it, kid."

Kiyoko lowered her head. "I am not worthy."

"Come and chill with Charlanne before the show," Belle said. "She's decided she's having an identity crisis and she needs to reinvent herself."

"She's not mad at *Flirt*?"

"Hell, yeah. She's thinking of suing *Flirt*," Belle replied. "Come on. We have champagne."

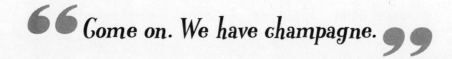

**" Come on. We have champagne. "**

6        6        6        6

It was eleven P.M., and the *Flirt* show was about to begin.

Mel stood backstage beside Bishop. The tall, thin woman with the tight black bun and ruby-red lips was dressed in a perfectly tailored tux. So were her department heads, and all her interns—even Liv and Gen, who were in the trenches, i.e., assisting with wardrobe and makeup. Kiyoko was in the sound booth with Belle and the mixing guys, plus a tiny army of sound guys sent in by all the different celebs.

Donato came up with his headset on, waiting for his cue to begin. Mel, who hadn't met him before, was very goosebumpy beside him. When he flashed a grin at her, she thought she might collapse in a puddle.

Then the gong sounded, and Donato said into his mike:

*"You want to be a VIP.*

*"You want to shimmer and shine; you want to be the one.*

*"You are."*

Then he broke into his signature song, "La Bella," and the first ten models moved from the wings and sailed down the runway. They were dressed in shifting tints of warm colors: apple red, persimmon, and tangerine. The fashions in this first set were created by some of the lesser-known designers Bishop had invited, and each designer walked beside his or her model, in a tux. Tall, short, dark, light, they all looked thrilled as they turned at the U of the runway, waving to the audience.

Donato stopped singing and said:

"*Your moment to shine. Your time. You are a VIP.*"

As the ten models and designers walked back up the runaway, Donato finished his song.

Mel knew lightning-fast changes were occurring in the sound booth as they mixed the output for their next "audio presenter," Kanye West.

ତ     ତ     ତ     ତ

Backstage, Liv stood back from Miko, who had been chosen to wear the Norwegian pelt dress, and nodded.

"You look brill."

Miko snorted. "I look like a cavewoman." Then she lost her smirk as the young Norwegian designer arrived to walk her down the aisle. He was tall and Nordic and half the models had a crush on him.

"You look so nice," he said in heavily accented English.

"*Takk,*" Miko replied, and he dimpled. Liv knew that was Norwegian for "thank you."

"Everyone ready?" Demetria asked. She had still not warmed back up to pre-earring levels of frostiness, but the need to work with split-second timing during the show had created a sort of truce between them.

"Yes, Demetria," Liv replied, gesturing to her ten models. "They're ready."

The gong sounded.

As Miko passed Liv, she said loudly, "I showed your earrings to Kate Moss last night. She wants a dozen pairs."

Then Miko swept out of the wings and down the runway.

ⓖ    ⓖ    ⓖ    ⓖ

In the sound booth, Kiyoko and Belle bopped to Kanye and smiled at each other.

Belle said, "I thought this would be hokey, but it's actually cool."

Kiyoko danced with her head. "You really smoothed things over with Charlanne. How do you do it?"

"Just a master," Belle drawled. "She just wanted to still be special, you know?"

"A VIP," Kiyoko rejoined.

"Yeah, not some wacko with a life-changing tattoo," Belle said.

They both cracked up.

"By the way, I invited a few talent men to the *Flirt*

bash after the show. They all got your CD, so don't give 'em any."

"Oh my God, I thought you were tired of being my mentor," Kiyoko confessed.

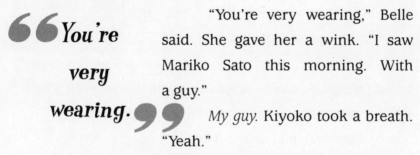 "You're very wearing," Belle said. She gave her a wink. "I saw Mariko Sato this morning. With a guy."

*My guy.* Kiyoko took a breath. "Yeah."

"A tall Japanese guy, and she was kissing him so hard I thought he would deflate."

"Oh." Kiyoko's brows shot up.

"Give Cody a call." Then Belle said to the sound guy at the mixing board, "Don't forget what we discussed. Lots of bass is what my baby likes."

☺ ☺ ☺ ☺

Gen adjusted the sleeves of her tux, looking on enviously as the makeup guy added just a dab of shine to Alexa's lips. No modeling for Gen. Liv stood beside Gen with a look of wonder on her face.

Heading the last set of ten models, Alexa was wearing the dress designed for Lily, the most famous supermodel on the planet. After several fittings to adjust it to Alexa's curvier body, Gianna had declared that it looked better on her than it ever would have on Lily.

Although she was still suing Lily . . .

"You look so beautiful," Liv said. She frowned slightly. "Don't cry, Alexa."

"I—I can't believe this," Alexa said.

"It's happening," Liv told her.

A few feet away, Trey and Charlotte waved from beside a digital camera setup. *Flirt* was sending out a live feed, and Electronic Content was in charge of it.

Alexa waved back at them.

The gong sounded. It was time.

"Here you go, Cinderella," Liv said. "Good luck, Alexa."

*"Muchas gracias,"* Alexa murmured.

She stepped into the glare of the spotlights and began walking. Appreciative murmurs gave way to applause as Alexa passed each set of front-row seats.

She kept walking, so nervous she was afraid she might fall off the runway and into the lap of—*Ay, Dios mio, is that El Torero?*

As she walked toward the U-turn, she heard Sting

> 66 *She kept walking, so nervous she was afraid she might fall off the runway and into the lap of—Ay, Dios mio, is that El Torero?* 99

saying, *"You want to be a VIP.*

*"You want to shimmer and shine, you want to be the one. You are."*

As she reached the end of the runway, showers of rose petals fluttered from the ceiling. The delighted audience started laughing and cheering.

She paused, blinded by the spotlights as the petals kissed her cheeks.

*"You are a VIP. You are, you are,"* Sting sang.

Then she turned back up the runway, joining the group. Soon everyone was crowding onstage, gathering around Bishop, applauding, too. Bishop, her arms filled with long-stemmed red roses, was loving it, smiling with those bloodred lips, and graciously accepting the accolades like the VIP she was.

All the models blew kisses at the audience, at one another, and at Bishop. More people in tuxes joined the crowd—these were the accessory designers, ranging from a famous Milanese shoe designer to a previously unknown South African, whose carved bone bracelet adorned Miko's wrist.

**"*Now we party!*"** Mel, Gen, and Liv joined the throng, and they waved at Charlotte in the wings and at Kiyoko, hidden away in the sound booth.

*My VIPs,* Alexa thought. *My dear friends. What will happen next to us Flirtistas?*

"Now we party!" Miko said into her ear. "And we talk about you and Paris!"

"Me and Paris?" Alexa echoed, startled.

"Oh, yes. I can get you launched in no time," Miko said. "You've been in the *Flirt* show, luv, in a Gianna Russo original."

The rose petals fluttered down like fairy dust.